VIRTUAL SILENCE

by
JOAN SCHWEIGHARDT

THE PERMANENT PRESS
Sag Harbor, New York 11963

for Adam and Alex

Copyright © 1995 by Joan Schweighardt

Library of Congress Cataloging-in-Publication Data

Schweighardt, Joan, 1949–
   Virtual silence / by Joan Schweighardt.
     p.   cm.
   ISBN 1-877946-61-3 : $22.00
   1. Teenage girls—New Jersey—Fiction. 2. Murder—New Jersey—
Fiction. I. Title.
PS3569.C568V57   1995
813'.54—dc20   94-29232
                                                        CIP

first edition, October—1500 copies

Manufactured in the United States of America

THE PERMANENT PRESS
Noyac Road
Sag Harbor, NY 11963

3 9510 2002 5211 5

Prologue

Even before the killings my disposition toward the opposite sex was something less than favorable, in part because of my father leaving, and in part because of the company I kept.

Sharon was a big girl with tiny brown eyes set deep into a pale fleshy face. Her father had died when she was three, and some years later she discovered his clothes in a trunk in the basement and took them over. By the time she was twelve, she was wearing his shirts over her jeans regularly in an effort to conceal her breasts, which were larger than she would have liked. Likewise, on all but the hottest days, she hid the rest of herself beneath the generous fabric of his old brown raincoat. She walked with a slight forward tilt, sliding her feet instead of lifting them. She was clumsy—the sight of her own shadow was enough to throw her off balance—and so eager to get where she was going that she could hardly round a corner without bumping into something. When she spoke, she threw her hands about, so that Terri and I were constantly moving her soda cans and milk cartons away from the edge of the table.

You could argue, I suppose, that her bias was a reaction to the fact that the opposite sex took virtually no interest in her, but that would be to imply that Sharon was somewhat shallow (a quality which she and Terri were fond of attributing to men), and that was anything but the case.

Sharon Michener was the most analytical person I had ever known; she was an investigator of procedure, a prober of the

3

essential. On the pretext of having to do research for school projects, for instance, she visited wineries (we had several in the area), saw mills, butchers' shops, hospitals, chemical companies, waste disposal plants, and, on a regular basis, our local UFO support group (though she had never had an encounter herself). She made frequent excursions into Manhattan to chat with the homeless. She visited convents, local prisons (of which we also had our share), nursing homes, dowsers' conventions—the list goes on. Sometimes she would invite Terri or me to accompany her, but more often she proceeded all on her own, by cab or bus if she could not get her mother's car, and we only heard about it later.

She had no time for "boys," she said. She had come to one school dance in our junior year, but that was only to see the headbangers in action, one of the few phenomena that did not hold her interest for long.

Terri was a voracious reader, particularly of philosophy, and whenever the subject of dating came up, she claimed, only half jokingly, to be saving herself for someone who fit Plato's description of the philosopher king—and we had no such creature in our high school. She was a small girl, not much bigger than myself, and she had to sit on a cushion when she drove her mother's huge Buick. She wore glasses, which she was constantly adjusting on her pert oily nose, and she had a way of drawing back her lips when she spoke so that you saw more teeth than you might have cared to. Her face was pleasantly freckled, and unlike Sharon, whose hair was stringy and unstyled, she used a blow-dryer each morning to discipline her otherwise unruly auburn curls. Boys were not particularly attracted to her either.

My acceptance of Sharon and Terri's conviction that men were shallow was based not on any direct observation but on Sharon and Terri themselves, for they were, in my opinion, the two most interesting people in our little hamlet of Rock Ridge, New York, and if the opposite sex failed to realize that, it could only be because they were content with surfaces. Terri was warm and gentle and had a contagious laugh, a kind of hee-hee-hee that she was able to negotiate with her teeth clamped together. She took a childlike delight in horses, sunny days, and animated Disney films. She was even-tempered, and always an earnest listener. (I can't tell you how supportive she was when my parents first separated.) Sharon was darker, sometimes grim, sometimes even confrontational. An avid *Star Trek* fan, she was more likely to greet people with Spock's hand salute than with a smile, but her mind was as full and as diverse as the Smithsonian.

What, you might wonder, did these two inwardly exquisite creatures see in me? Well, as Terri's mother, who was a Realtor, used to say, location is everything. (Sharon would argue that it was memory, while Terri said it was art. I had no opinion at the time, but now I would say that timing is; timing is everything.)

Rock Ridge was located in the foothills of the Catskills, and at one time its heavily wooded acres were broken up only by an occasional vacation cottage or dairy farm. But when the profit went out of farming, the owners subdivided both the farms and the land surrounding them, and the resulting lots were purchased by folks from New Jersey, like my parents, or from the City, like Terri's and Sharon's. Still, Rock Ridge remained quite rural, and unless you were living right in the village, the homes were spread out on winding back roads with acres of woods in between. Terri and Sharon and I were thrown together as children simply because we were the same sex, the same age, and within biking distance of one another.

I amused them, if anything. They said I talked too much. I was still playing with dolls when Sharon's mother began to teach them to play chess. In fact, my dolls were present at some of their earliest tournaments, and they watched the games with a perseverance which I could only admire. Not that Sharon didn't make good use of my attention deficit. She would send me off to the kitchen for snacks when she got hungry, or to the radio to scan for a better station. I was useful; I kept track of their scores. And sometimes when their games were over, one of them would consent to play a game of checkers with me.

Sometimes entire weeks passed without us getting together. Even before she got her license, Sharon's investigations took up much of her time. If she had no money for a cab and couldn't persuade her mother to take her where she wanted to go, she would set off on foot for the woods behind her house in search of deer and the small changes that occurred along the stream between storms.

This didn't faze Terri in the least—as long as she had something good to read, and her definition of "good" was expansive. (Although the Taylors had no pets, I once found her engrossed in a dog-training manual.) But I grew bored and lonely during those times. I would pace near the telephone, cursing my two friends for having minds in which they could actually live. On paper, which is to say report cards, you could not tell us apart, but that was only because I worked twice as hard as either of them. The truth was that my mind drifted as aimlessly as an abandoned boat. It was as content to peruse glossy magazine advertisements as it was to acknowledge brief moments of comprehension, or, less often, inspiration, when they came along. In my efforts at discipline, I took up my father's suggestion and began violin lessons when I was twelve, but I was never very good. Then, thinking that a venture into the world of gymnastics might benefit me, I got my mother to buy me a small trampoline. I made good use of it over the years, but jumping did not strengthen my mind as much as relax it when *it* had been jumping.

I might have made other friends. Unlike Sharon and Terri, I knew how to respond to the other girls in school when they showed me the little paintings on the tips of their fingernails or described the outfits they had seen at the mall. But I didn't—not because I feared that Sharon and Terri would be upset with me for reaching out beyond our little circle, but because I feared that they might not.

Strangely enough, it was Sharon who eventually made another friend.

This was in our junior year. We had been studying Shakespeare's *Julius Caesar* in our honors English class, and the element of persuasion that runs through the play dominated much of our conversation even after we had had our test and moved on to *Romeo and Juliet*. "Do you see how Cassius proceeds?" Sharon asked Terri and me in the cafeteria one day. She had her text opened on the table beside her brown bag lunch and was so animated that she even spoke with her mouth full, so that we were forced to consider, along with her words, the sight of her pink tongue probing her teeth for soggy lumps of white bread. "He flatters Brutus first, and then, when he sees how attached Brutus is to his 'honor,' he uses the word as a cloak beneath which both men can vent their petty grievances." She looked aside for a moment, in disgust. "So here we have a basically good but shallow man who is flattered into thinking that Cassius' cause and his honor are somehow linked. . . ."

She loved the play, and so certain was she that our peers could learn a thing or two from it that she went to the drama department and asked Mr. Muddle to consider putting it on that spring in lieu of *South Pacific.* He agreed, reluctantly, to put it on in addition to the musical, but only if Sharon would rewrite, both cut and transform it into the vernacular, hence, mutilate it, Sharon said. But she consented, and the three of us spent most of that long, snowy winter in Sharon's bedroom, which was wall-papered with maps from *National Geographic,* bickering over the project.

Naturally, I was anxious to attend opening night. But Sharon, who by then was somewhat ashamed of our effort, had to be dragged, literally, from her house. Terri and I had to march in and take away her bowl of popcorn and pull her away from the documentary she had been watching on the TV and drape her ragged brown raincoat over her shoulders and lead her, not kicking and screaming but twisting to see the denouement on the TV screen, to Terri's mother's car.

We sat in the back of the auditorium, away from the few others who had bothered to come, with Sharon slumped down in her seat between us. She was quiet and so preoccupied with her own thoughts that she didn't even complain when Terri and I leaned in toward each other, commenting on the cast that Mr. Muddle had chosen. But then an incredible thing happened. Portia appeared on the stage, saying, "Brutus, my lord," one of the few lines that we had left intact.

Beverly Sturbridge was an earnest student, a hard worker like myself. We knew her; she was in our English class. But she had a frivolous side (always laughing, always smiling— you know the type), and I don't think any of us was prepared for the elegance that she lent to the speech that followed. "You left my bed, Brutus," she said, her dark eyes flaming. "And last night in the middle of dinner you got up and paced, sighing the way you do when you're upset. And when I tried to talk to you, you lifted your hand. . . ."

Sharon sat up and lifted her own hand, a warning for Terri and me to quiet down. By the time Portia pulled up her dress to reveal her wounded thigh, Sharon was literally hanging over the back of the seat in front of her, mumbling, "She's very good, very good."

When the play was over, we went backstage, for the purpose, or so I thought, of congratulating Beverly on her fine portrayal. But before either Terri or I could open our mouths, Sharon began an apology that was more sincere than any of the speeches (excepting Beverly's, of course) that we had heard in the play itself. "We were told to cut the play and change the language," she cried, incriminating Terri and me with a backward sweep of her arm. "And we consented, because, well . . . we wanted to have *some* semblance of an audience. But now I realize we did you a great disservice. I can imagine how wonderful you would have been if you had been able to speak Shakespeare's own words!"

God only knows what Beverly had thought of us before. For my own part, I could not remember her ever having said more to me than, "What did you get on *your* paper?" She was an assertive girl, and as comfortable flirting with the jocks as she was reading her mediocre essays aloud in English class. She had a multitude of friends and couldn't have needed three more. But she was also an aspiring actress, and as susceptible to Sharon's flattery as Brutus had been to Cassius'. And so the courtship began.

To please Sharon, Bev learned Portia's true lines and delivered them the following week for us on the auditorium stage after school. "Riveting, absolutely riveting," Sharon said. The week after that, the three of us were invited to her house, where we met her parents and her brothers and then spent an hour in her bedroom talking theater. Whenever the phone rang, which was approximately every three minutes, we took stock of our surroundings—Degas prints on lavender walls, lavender canopied bed, white teddy bear collection.

She had a boyfriend, Jack the Jock, she called him (Sharon called him Jack the Joke behind her back), who played quarterback for the Rock Ridge football team. And because she saw him every weekend, we could not spend as much time with her as Sharon would have liked. Sharon, however, was as persevering as a puppy, and when Bev invited us to sit at her table in the cafeteria, she agreed wholeheartedly. Previously, the three of us had always sat at a table in the back of the cafeteria near the trash cans. Because of the smell, no one else sat in the area. Yet everyone had to pass the trash cans, and thus our table, on their way out. Sharon liked to point out that this afforded us the opportunity to speak with our classmates when we wanted to without the burden of committing ourselves to an entire lunch period with them.

Bev's table, and that was what it was always called, was right in the middle of the cafeteria. Every seat was filled, and the spillover sat at the tables before and behind. The first time Bev brought us over there, saying, "You all know Sharon and Terri and Ginny," her friends, both male and female, nodded and then pretended that we weren't there for the duration of the meal. But after a week or so, they grew accustomed to our presence and even began to make eye contact with us as they gossiped or told their amusing anecdotes. I fit right in, I found, and before long I was telling my own amusing stories. One of the boys, a little too loud for my tastes, even asked me out, and another, who I would have gone out with *had* he asked, hinted that I was next in line when he and the girl he was currently dating broke up.

Terri did not fare as well. She smiled a lot, but she was shy, and if someone spoke to her directly, a blush arose from her collar, which she seemed to think she could subdue by blinking a lot. Sharon said little too, but this was not from awkwardness. She was content to listen to Bev talk, to watch her laugh, to see her mouth fall open in surprise or horror. In short, Bev's existence had become the object of Sharon's acute analysis.

Except for that one time in her bedroom and the one afternoon when Bev delivered Portia's true lines, we never saw her alone again until the day of the killings. But we accompanied her and her entourage to several after-school events—baseball games, pep rallies, casual gatherings in the town park. And I was happy, for I felt I had attained the best

9

of both worlds. I had a large circle of, if not friends, at least acquaintances, and I had not had to give up Sharon and Terri in the bargain. Then summer came, and it was just the three of us again.

Bev's parents had a vacation home up in Maine, on the coast. Before she left, Bev gave Sharon the number, and Sharon called her weekly. Whenever Terri and I asked for a report on her activities, Sharon would look aside for a moment and smile dreamily before answering, as if to savor the emotion her name evoked. Bev was swimming, shelling, hiking, working on her tan. In the evenings she attended parties. On the weekends, Jack came up to visit her in the little red Honda his parents had bought him for his birthday.

We heard from one of Bev's friends at the beginning of the summer. Heather called, me specifically, to invite us to a party, but of course Sharon didn't want to go. I might have argued with her, insisted that a healthier rapport with Bev's friends could only enhance our reunion with her in the fall, but I knew that Sharon would fail to see the logic in that. She was working on a one-woman play, which, she felt certain, Bev would ultimately perform. It was a sort of female version of the Faust legend in which Mephistopheles would be invisible to all but Bev—or Corina, the name that Sharon had chosen for her character. She wouldn't let us see it, but she assured us that Bev was very excited about it.

With Sharon writing and Terri reading—*Faust* and *Doctor Faustus,* for Sharon's project had got her interested too—our get-togethers were not only infrequent but as gloomy as you might expect. Sharon and Terri could discuss the notion of selling one's soul to the devil quite objectively, but these conversations frightened me, and there were many nights when I woke up sweating and thinking that some *thing* was in my room, in addition to Surge, my dog, who shared it with me. For once, I was happy not to be in their company. I had just got my driver's license, so I spent time driving my mother's ridiculous Yugo around, but as she needed it for work, it was not as often as I would have liked. In the hope of getting my own car, I sought employment, but had no success. I visited my father, read a few books from our summer reading list, and lay around the house—on the sofa or out in the back on my mother's chaise longue—wondering what would happen in the fall when Bev returned and our senior year began.

Had I had a crystal ball, I would have packed my bags and gone as far away from Rock Ridge as I could possibly get.

1

My mother was on the floor, rummaging through the laundry basket. She was wearing only underwear—green cotton panties and a purple athletic bra—with one pink sock draped over her shoulder like a dish towel. She located its mate, examined the two together, and muttering something about destitution, threw both socks aside disgustedly. I could see that my timing wasn't very good, but then that is the essence of my story. "Ma," I began.

Without turning, she withdrew her hands from the basket just long enough to flutter them at the sides of her head. "Not . . . now," she advised, leaving a gap between the words for emphasis.

I went to my room and dug out a pair of good woolen socks that I'd been saving for winter—a major sacrifice, because when she returned from her Tai Chi class, where they trained in stockinged feet, the socks would be in as bad shape as all of hers. When I came back to the kitchen, the floor was littered with threadbare socks, one of which Surge had begun to chew. "Ma," I said again.

This time she turned, and I saw that her eyes were moist. It didn't take much to set her off these days. I held the socks out to her, but it took a moment for her expression to soften. "I've never seen those before," she whispered.

If I told her that Dad had bought them for me, she'd refuse to wear them, so I mumbled something about having inherited them from Jill, Terri's older sister who had moved to Texas over the summer. Hesitantly, she reached toward my outstretched hand, but just as her fingers were about to make contact, I jerked mine back—not far, just enough to let her know that there was more going on here than a simple act of charity. The brief display of bewilderment that appeared on her face made my heartbeat quicken. "I need to borrow twenty bucks," I said briskly. "I'll pay you back as soon as I find a job."

Her hand withdrew in haste. "No!" she snapped. "If you couldn't find a job over the summer, how do you expect to find one now?"

"I tried!" I whined.

She was on her feet, tilting toward the basement door. She must have known I'd follow, because she kept right on talking. "You call that trying? What'd you make, three phone calls? Four? If you'd really *wanted* to find employment, you would have by now. You should be ashamed, a girl your age."

As we hurried down the stairs and turned toward the washer, I had to bite my lip to keep from reminding her of how long it had taken her to find her job, as a receptionist in a local insurance agency. "This is really important," I pleaded.

She opened the lid and weeded through the dirty clothes within until she finally came up with the same pair of blue socks that she had worn to Bingo the week before. She held them up and inspected them for holes. "The answer is no. I'm not even going to ask what you want it for," she said.

That was best, because I wasn't prepared to tell her. "Well, can you at least drop me at Dad's on your way out? And pick me up on your way back again? Maybe *he* can spare a few dollars."

She lifted the socks to her nose, sniffed, jerked her head back in response, then shrugged and bent to slip them on anyway. She turned from the machine and, having had a second thought, spun back around to pour some powder in and start it up. Then she squared up her shoulders, brought her hands up in front of her face, and crossed them with her palms facing her. Slowly, and with her eyes empty and her lips pursed in concentration, she raised one knee to her chest, then kicked, Tai Chi fashion. I couldn't be sure whether her imaginary adversary was Dad or me, but whoever it was, she must have imagined a reaction to her assault too, because she smiled. "Sure," she said, stepping past me. "Just be sure that you're out by the Dumpsters at eight sharp. I'm not going in to get you."

At the top of the stairs we ran off in different directions, she towards her bedroom to finish dressing and I towards mine to answer the phone. "Did you get it yet?" Sharon asked. "I'm still trying," I confessed and hung up.

Dad's tiny kitchen smelled of burnt meat. They'd been separated for nearly a year, and he still hadn't learned to cook. "Ginny! Come in," he said, even though I'd already closed the door and was standing with my back to it. I knew he'd have preferred me to knock, but if I didn't have to announce my entries into my mother's house, I didn't see why I should when I came to his apartment. I had talked it over with Terri, and we had concluded that it was my duty as their daughter to insure that both the pleasures and the drawbacks of parenting remained equally distributed in spite of their split.

He was smiling his closed-lipped smile, and it occurred to me that almost all the adults I knew smiled that way. It was the kind of smile that could have hidden anything, a formality more than a genuine response to delight. He was sitting at the table. Clustered before him were the tools of his trade: computer, books, paper, pencils, ashtray, smokes, matches, and beer bottle. At the far end was his dinner plate, a blackened steak bone in the middle of it. As there were no other food scraps, I assumed he'd either had a single-serving dinner or literally licked the plate clean. "Can I take that home for Surge?" I asked.

"Sure," he said. "Sit down. Tell me how your mother's doing."

I looked past him, at the gray Formica counter. Except for the microwave, which had come with the apartment, there wasn't a single thing on it. I thought of the counter space at home, cluttered so tightly with food processors and coffee pots and canisters, so many various trinkets that "space" was hardly the word to define it. "She went out tonight wearing a pair of dirty socks that she took from a load of laundry that had been sitting in the washer for a week," I said.

His smile elongated. This was the kind of thing he liked

to hear. It confirmed that he had used good sense in allowing her to throw him out. I only stooped that low when I wanted something, but he hadn't caught on to that yet. If she was the bad guy, then he had to be the good guy. It rendered him more inclined to give in to my requests. I might have gone on about her, mentioned that she seldom made her bed anymore or that she hadn't read a newspaper in over a month, but I didn't have time to beat around the bush. "How's your financial situation?" I asked.

He let his eyes drift down to the computer screen, not a favorable indication. "Didn't your mother get my last check?"

"Yes, but we had to use it all up on school clothes. Then this other thing came up."

I hesitated. Sharon had called just after dinner to inform me that tomorrow was the day; I hadn't had time to formulate a decent fabrication. Then something hit me. "I broke a string on my violin," I said.

He looked up at me. I lifted my chin and smiled his tight smile right back at him. We both knew I practiced the violin as infrequently as possible; in fact, I hadn't had a lesson in well over a year. Still, it was he who had started me on it, he who had insisted that it would round me out, make me the target of more college solicitations than I could imagine. And it was his lies to my mother that had gotten him thrown out; he was in no position to risk an accusation.

He puffed out his cheeks and exhaled, a trace of smoke from his cigarette emerging with his breath. "Okay," he said. "Okay."

He got up from the table, wiped his hands on his back pockets, and left the room. I leaned over immediately to see what was happening on his computer. He was in his word-processing program, but there was only one line on the screen: *She moved across the deck in the dark. Shit!* I didn't know whether the expletive was part of the text or only his reaction to it. Starting was always tough for him. He'd rewrite first chapters for months on end before he got the tone and tempo the way he wanted. Once he got through that though, his books were as good as done. This one was going to be an historical novel about some pirates. I didn't know much about pirates myself, except that they were a superstitious lot and would rather take their chances swimming with the sharks than to sail with a woman on board. It figured that my father would feel compelled to go against the grain and insert one in there anyway.

He gave me five bucks more than I'd hoped for and offered to make me a cup of tea, which I declined. Then, thinking that I should compensate him for the money, I began to tell him all about my first week of school. I described each of my teachers, exaggerating their eccentricities so as to get him to laugh. But he didn't; he just smiled and nodded his head.

I looked at the clock, and seeing that it was almost eight, I mumbled something about Mom coming for me and got out of my chair. Uncharacteristically, he got up too, to see me to the door. "So, when will you be coming by again?" he asked.

I stepped halfway out and stared down the catwalk, considering. My eye fell on the woman who had just emerged from the stairs at the end. It was just getting dark, so I couldn't make out her features very well, but what caught my attention was her size. Being so small myself (one of Bev's friends had told me that I could pass for an eighth-grader), I had always been interested in people of uncommon stature. This lady was practically a giant. But you could tell by the way she walked—hips swinging, longish hair bouncing from side to side—that she liked herself that way.

My father had been staring at Goliath too, but he dropped his gaze abruptly when I turned to tell him that I'd probably stop by over the weekend. Then he put his hand on my back and said that it had been nice to see me. He didn't exactly push me out, but there was some pressure in his fingertips, which, in my confusion, I responded to.

I walked some twenty feet and then looked back over my shoulder. Dad was no longer at the door, but the ribbon of light there confirmed that he had left it slightly opened. When I turned back again, the woman was just in front of me. She was wearing faded red leggings and a purple V-necked sweater over a white turtleneck. Her shoulder bag was enormous. "Hello," she said.

I smiled one of my father's throw-away smiles and picked

up my pace. There were only two apartments after his, and I didn't remember either of them having their outside lights on. The woman's footsteps ceased. I listened for voices but heard none. I didn't hear any knocking either.

When I arrived home, I got my trampoline out from beneath the bed and began to bounce. My father, the way I saw it, had no right to a private life, or at least not one so private that it excluded me. What, I wondered, was in Goliath's bag? Toiletries and a change of clothes for tomorrow? The phone rang, and I went down on my knees and bounced up again with the receiver. I told Sharon that I had gotten the money and would see her in the morning.

I jumped and reviewed our visit several times over. At first I was inclined to give Dad the benefit of the doubt. Goliath's arrival might have been a surprise to him, too, in which case his not mentioning it made perfect sense. Then I remembered that he had offered me tea, which, except when I was sick, I never drank. He must have realized that. Had he offered me a soda, which he always had on hand, I would have said yes. Then I might have stayed a little longer, given him more details about my classes. It wouldn't have been the first time I'd let Mom sit in the car and stew.

The light went off in the living room, signaling that Mom was going to bed. "Get your homework finished?" she asked as she passed my door. The question was reflexive and required no response.

I jumped harder to increase my altitude, until I was almost touching the ceiling. Jumping Ginny, my father used to call me, but that was back in the days when he was still computer illiterate, back when he still moved from room to room when he needed something and was, therefore, apt to pass my door and take note of me.

Ironically, Mom bought him his first computer as an anniversary present. She might just as well have introduced him to the sexiest woman she knew. He was seduced immediately, and being an organizer by nature, he spent months on end transferring not only his manuscripts, but all his personal records into tidy, accessible computer files. Mom complained, because he seldom left his home office during this time, but he assured her that once he had completed his task—and, with his documents at his fingertips!—he'd have all the time in the world for her. But then he upgraded and went on-line.

Instead of going to the library, where Mom had often accompanied him, to do his research, he began to do it over the Internet. He stopped reading the newspaper, which he and Mom had liked to share, because he could get the news faster on his modem. Computer forums enabled him to parley with fellow hackers. However, being a private man, he preferred one to one "conversations" via electronic mail. It was in this manner that he met Prissy Walker, the woman with whom he had the affair. Nothing would have come of it, he told Mom later, if it hadn't turned out that she lived only forty miles away.

We had had a talk some time ago, after the affair had ended, and he had implied that he was just waiting for time to pass, that his long-range objective was to wiggle his way back into my mother's affection. I had no reason at the time to think he was equivocating.

Surge nosed my door open and came in to lie down on the rug at the foot of my bed. He was old now, slow and cautious. Even the act of settling himself for sleep appeared to take some effort. Watching him, I realized that I had forgotten the bone I'd meant to bring him. I had been ushered out of Dad's apartment that fast.

2

It was sticky in the morning. The sky was gray and there were gnats flying around my head. A faint breeze stirred the leaves of Mom's neglected tomato plants as I waited for Sharon and Terri to pick me up in Terri's mother's Buick. Bev was taking the bus to school and we were to meet her out on the lot. There was some danger involved; there was always the chance that one of our teachers might see us leaving. But the episode with my father had kept me awake half the night, and I was in a risk-taking mood and looked forward to a near escape.

Our timing, however, was meticulous. Bev's bus was just unloading as we pulled into the lot. She saw us, nodded solemnly, and walked toward the corner of the building. We made the turn and stopped just long enough for her to slip into the back seat. Then we continued around the building and exited from the rear lot. A moment later we were coasting south on 402, heading for the highway. "Where to?" Terri asked.

"The City? The Met?" I offered. We cut school infrequently, only three or four times a year. It seemed a shame to risk an ISS—an In School Suspension—on anything less.

"That works for me," Terri said, adjusting her glasses.

I turned to look at the other two. Sharon, who was wearing her raincoat in spite of the heat, was staring out the window, at the rolling green pastures, a dreamer's smile at play on her lips. She had informed me the day before, quite uncharacteristically, that she didn't care where we went. Clearly, she was only too happy to be in Bev's company. Bev, however, was sitting forward, her mouth opened, her tongue pushing against the back of her lower lip. I turned around again. "Bev doesn't want to go to the City," I told Terri.

"Whatever," Terri said, glancing in the rear-view. "Where do you want to go then, Bev?"

"New Jersey," Bev said, and she sat back as if to indicate that she would tolerate no challenge on the issue.

"New Jersey!" I exclaimed. Even Sharon, whose dazed expression usually didn't evaporate until noon, turned her head from the window to cast an astonished eye on her.

"I've got a reason," Bev said defensively.

"A reason to go to New Jersey? That's an oxymoron," Sharon mumbled, but she smiled lest Bev should think her critical.

"There are malls in New Jersey," Bev continued. "I want to go to one of them, I don't care which. There's something I have to buy. Let's get out of the area and then stop for something to eat. Then I promise to tell you all about it." She shot a glance at Sharon. "It's something *very* serious; I don't want to talk about it in the car."

Silence followed. What else could have succeeded a declaration like that? We stopped for gas, Bev and Sharon and I each handing over a five to Terri so that she could fill up the tank. When we started off again, I put down the visor and popped open the plastic cover on the mirror, ostensibly to see what shape my hair was in. I moved the visor around until I had Bev in my view. She was looking down at her lap, where her hands were neatly folded.

Since school had begun, I'd noticed a change in her. She'd been herself in the cafeteria—which is to say at the center of things—cheerfully describing her adventures in Maine, the seals she'd encountered, the people she'd met, the volleyball games on the beach, and so forth. But I'd come upon her in the bathroom the day before and found her staring at her reflection as if it were a stranger's, so intent on her own thoughts that she didn't even notice me behind her until I said hello. And I'd seen her later in the hall with her head bent, until Jack appeared at her side and took her arm. Sharon had told her last spring that we cut school a few times during the course of the year. Though Bev had listened enthusiastically, she had given no indication that she had any interest in joining us. Yet it was *she* who had approached *us* about this particular escapade. When Terri had said that we usually waited until after the first quarter, by which time our teachers had come to trust us, Bev argued that there was no better time than now, when our teachers were still laying out their curriculum.

I put the visor back up and tried to imagine what she could possibly have on her mind. Her parents were wealthy and together. Sharon was writing a play for her, and Mr. Muddle had already offered her the lead in the school play. Jack had a job and a car and sent her roses every month to commemorate their anniversary. Her skin tanned the moment she stepped outdoors, and the platinum streaks in her hair, which she had acquired even before she left for Maine, looked as though they would prevail all winter long. I concluded that she either had cancer or was pregnant and made some attempt to forgive her for the somber mood that had taken hold in the car.

We took the highway to the end and paid the toll to get onto the thruway. It couldn't be cancer, I realized. Bev's mother had driven her in to school the first day, and Sharon, who had waited outside for her, had commented later about how cheerfully Mrs. Sturbridge had greeted her. It was as unlikely that Bev could have cancer without her mother knowing it as it was that Mrs. Sturbridge could know it and still be cheerful. That left being pregnant, but now that I'd had some miles to think about it, that didn't seem a possibility either. Bev was smart, cautious, and had mentioned once that she was on the pill. More likely she had had a fight with Jack, and *that* was what she needed so desperately to talk about. If she wanted to go shopping, it was probably to get some trinket to appease him.

Just past the "Welcome to New Jersey" sign we had our first hazy glimpse of the City off in the distance. I pointed it out, thinking that it still wasn't too late to alter our destination. "The trouble with us is that we have no sense of adventure," I declared, rising above the temptation to exclude Sharon and Terri and myself from the "us." "We can talk anywhere. We can park the car in a lot and take a subway to the Met. Sharon loves subways, don't you, Shar? Or we could get on the parkway, drive down to the New Jersey shore, do our talking while we're scouting out beached whales and medical supplies in the surf."

"We're taking a risk," Terri said softly, keeping her eyes on the traffic. "We're cutting classes."

Sharon barked a laugh. "Some risk," she said. "I don't know about you guys, but my mother is always so overwhelmed by my grades that she never even looks to see how many days I was absent."

"I got a C last year," Terri said.

Sharon sat as far forward as her seat belt would permit. "Oh yeah? You never told me. In what?"

"AP calc."

Everyone laughed, even Bev. I sat back in my seat, proud to have broken the spell. I had stuff to talk about too. Since I'd gotten up, I'd been rehearsing what I was going to say to my friends about Dad and Goliath. Like Bev, I was just waiting until we got some place where we could see one other's faces. But that didn't mean we had to sacrifice the entire day. "There's a diner coming up," I said. "Let's get something to eat and then see if we want to reevaluate our plans."

I figured Bev was upset with me, so I avoided making eye contact with her as we got out of the car and approached the long glass-and-concrete building. In fact, I was so preoccupied with how I was going to sell the idea of the City to Terri, who would have the final word, that I tripped on a crack in the walkway and went down on my knees. Terri and Sharon laughed and kept walking. I assumed the tug on my arm was Bev, who had been walking just behind me, but when I looked up, I saw that it was a man.

"Are you all right, young lady?" he asked. His features were so crumpled with concern that his glasses slid down and he had to thumb them back up his nose.

"Yeah, I'm fine," I answered, embarrassed.

Sharon and Terri had stopped by the glass door. "She's fine," Sharon said. "She's a gymnast. She knows just how to fall."

As the man reluctantly released my arm, his wife stepped up over the curb to stand at his side. "A gymnast?" she asked. She had a pinched nose and gray-streaked, blunt-cut hair.

I shook my head. "She's teasing me."

"Oh," the woman said, her sudden smile bright against New Jersey's smog. "Because our daughter was a gymnast when she was your age."

I wondered what age she thought I was.

"She's gone now," the husband added. "We just took her up to college in Vermont last weekend." He had been smiling, but the moment he concluded his sentence his nostrils flared and his lips began to decline. I saw him lift one hand as if to cover his face, but then he regained control and lowered it again.

"He's a softy," his wife explained.

Sharon and Terri stood back and let the couple go in first. They glanced at the "Please seat yourself" sign, smiled at us over their shoulders, and headed off to the left. Terri was about to follow them when Sharon elbowed her, cocking her head in the other direction. "The last thing we need is some nosy adults who just said good-bye to their baby asking us why we aren't in school today," she whispered.

Something about the man's softness had struck a chord in me. Bev should have had the floor first, of course, but as she reached for her menu the moment we sat down, I took the opportunity to tell my companions all about Goliath and how my father had tried to push me out the door before she arrived. Bev and Sharon studied their menus while I spoke, but Terri removed her glasses to look at me. "What have we got here?" she asked. "He offered you tea, he didn't laugh when you described your teachers, he got up to see you to the door, and he put his hand on your back as you were saying good-bye. Personally, I think you're reading too much into it. If he'd invited her over, he would have said something as soon as you came—"

"No, you don't know how he operates—"

"Then, if he was trying to keep it from you, he would have shown some sign of nervousness, like looking at the clock every couple of minutes. I say it was a surprise visit, *if* it was a visit at all. Besides, she doesn't sound like your father's type."

Sharon laughed, her brown eyes twinkling in her fleshy face. "How would you know her father's type?"

23

"Her mother's small, and that computer woman was practically a midget," Terri said seriously.

Sharon laughed again and shook her head, rubbing her thumb over one eyelid. Ordinarily I would have been offended, but I found myself forgiving her levity because I knew that it had more to do with Bev being with us than with anything else. She put her menu down and cleared her throat. "What do you say about all this, Bev?" she asked.

Bev studied first Sharon and then me over the top of her menu, her dark eyes steady and expressionless. She hesitated for so long that I began to think she would go back to her menu without saying a single word. Then she licked her upper lip. "Did you mention the woman to your mother?" she asked.

"No."

"Why not?"

"Because I wasn't sure. I wouldn't tell her something like that unless I was certain."

"You weren't sure. Your father's allowed to have friends, isn't he? Maybe it was someone who lives downstairs coming up to loan him a book or something."

"She had more than a book in that bag of hers."

"Is there a laundry room at his end of the catwalk? Or some kind of a storage area?"

I shrugged, though in fact, there was a laundry room. I had forgotten all about that.

"Maybe she was going in there. You said you didn't see where she went. Maybe she had laundry in her bag. I don't even know why we're discussing this anyway. You're his daughter, not his wife. It's really none of your business, is it?" And she disappeared behind her menu again.

Dumbfounded, I looked to Sharon and Terri for help. Sharon's eyes shone with the prospect of a confrontation, but Terri, ever the peacemaker, shook her head and dropped her gaze to her menu. I thought I knew what she was thinking. We had crossed the line with one another over the years, many times, but we didn't really even know Bev. She was Sharon's acquisition, and although Sharon herself didn't seem to think that my behavior could sabotage their relationship, Terri clearly thought otherwise. Not that she cared much about Bev except for Sharon's sake.

The waitress, a heavyset young woman with a high brown ponytail, appeared at our table and asked if we had made up our minds. While she took the others' orders, I scanned the other side of the diner and located the man and his wife. They were in a booth, sitting not across from each other but side by side, as if they'd left the other seat empty to commemorate the memory of their daughter. The man picked up his coffee cup, but before he sipped, he said something to his wife that made her toss her head back. Her nostrils were long and narrow above her smile. Then he said something else, and this time she laughed outright and elbowed him. His eyes widened, and he looked down to his lap, where a drop of his coffee had apparently spilled. He pointed it out to her and she shook her head good-humoredly and made some comment, probably about him being a slob. He considered her comment for a moment, then leaned over to say something directly into her ear. It might have been erotic, because she lifted her brows and offered him a devious smile.

"Wake up," Sharon said.

The waitress was glaring at me, the tip of her pen pressed into her pad. "Eggs," I said quickly.

They loved each other, that was clear. They were older than my parents and not nearly as good-looking. The woman was too thin and prim-looking in her old-fashioned gray suit, and she could have used a little makeup. The man was flabby and bald, and his eyes either bulged or appeared to because of the thickness of his glasses which, being framed in black, didn't help matters. But their daughter was off somewhere in Vermont, starting college with the full knowledge—or so I thought—that when she came home for Thanksgiving, her parents would still be together.

"And how would you like them done?" There was an edge in the waitress's voice. Her head was cocked and her chin was tucked back into her neck.

"I don't know. Scrambled," I said—a little sharply, I suppose, because Terri gave me a reproachful look.

She put her hand out to collect our menus, and as I was handing mine over, I noticed an entry for pancakes with strawberries and whipped cream. I hadn't even looked at the menu until then. "Miss," I said, but she was already turning and either hadn't heard me or was pretending she hadn't.

I would have called her again, but she moved to the table to the left of ours and started taking the orders there. I kept my eye on her, waiting for her to finish. The more I thought about it, the more fervently I wanted to change my order. Mom and I would be spending Thanksgiving either with my grandmother in Florida or, if at home, with the first person who invited us. My father would probably nuke a TV dinner and watch the football game with Goliath. Bev's words had stung me and the waitress had been rude to me. I wasn't about to settle for anything less than what I wanted. "Miss," I said again.

She couldn't have heard me. But I had been watching her back so intensely that it took an instant for the shot to register, and when I saw her shoulders tense, I thought at first she had. Unable to move my head, or any other part of my body for that matter, I watched in horror as the back of her blouse began to darken. I saw her pad and pencil slip from her hand. When she went down, I saw the man, the one who had helped me to my feet, the one who I had secretly wished had been my father. His mouth was wide open, poised for laughter, as if he could not conceive of this as being anything other than a joke. His head began to bob. I wanted to shout out to him, to tell him to close his mouth, to stop bobbing his head. I wanted to scream that he was too vulnerable with his head bobbing like that, too foolish-looking to go unnoticed. But when the next shot rang out, it was his wife who slumped.

Then I went down.

I took stock of myself. It seemed a few seconds passed before I was certain that my arrival on the floor had been self-motivated. I saw their legs, Terri's and Sharon's and Bev's. I tugged at Terri's, whose were nearest. She was just sliding down beside me when I saw Bev's legs fly up in the air and hit the underside of the table. Her chair tipped and went over. I couldn't see her face.

There were two more shots, then screams, then, I don't know how much later, whispered queries, shouted orders, sirens in the distance. Someone tried to lift me up but couldn't manage it. Someone draped a sweater around my shoulders. Someone, maybe the same person, whispered, "He's dead. He shot himself. It's over." But although I couldn't say whether the Samaritan's voice was male or female, I recognized with certainty the fear in it, and I knew that it was not over, that it would never be over.

3

I didn't see Sharon and Terri the next two days. We were all in shock and spent our time being catered to by our families. Together again at the funeral, we stood at the rear of a tremendous crowd, Sharon in the middle, erect and unflinching, pressing us to her sides as if we were children she meant to protect. It was drizzling that day, and of course she had on her brown raincoat. She held me so close that I could feel the wad of tissues she always kept handy in her pocket. But she didn't need them; she didn't cry.

The principal sought us out, to say that he would understand if we waited until Monday to return to school. I knew this only because Mom, whose doctor had prescribed some medication for me, related the information afterwards. But I took the last of the near-coma-inducing pills on Sunday, and by Monday, I was ready to talk about the event that had necessitated them. Mom, who hadn't left my side, agreed to call her office and ask for yet another day off. On Tuesday, I had her call in again, and her boss, who of course knew about everything, told her to take as much time as she needed.

I spent my days following her from room to room, talking frantically while she cleaned out closets she had never taken note of before and sucked on the plastic cigarettes she had substituted for the real thing some months back. I described the event, or at least my perception of it, over and over again, and begged her to help me make sense of it. I informed her of the ambivalence I had felt towards Bev, the guilt I now felt as a result of it. I talked about death generally, crime generally, the prospect of an afterlife, the process of decomposition, and a hundred other terrible things that seemed to be connected. At first she was kind, and when I burst into fresh tears, she would stop what she was doing and hold me, whispering reassurances into my ear. But after several days had passed—when all the closets in the house had been set to order, when the floors shone and the marks on the walls had been wiped away—I could see that I was getting on her nerves. "I don't have any answers for you," she said. "Maybe it's best to consider therapy when something like this happens."

I spent the evenings on the telephone, talking to Terri and Sharon, both of whom had opted to return to school the Monday after the funeral. Sharon was strangely matter-of-fact. The first few days, she reported, were nearly intolerable, with teachers and students alike bursting into tears in the corridors or in the middle of classes. The flag was still flying at half-mast, and the principal had called an assembly to talk about Bev and her academic contributions. But there had been so many sniffles and sobs in the auditorium that he broke down himself, and then the students sat for the rest of the period watching him weep into the palms of his hands. Boys and girls who had not even known Bev approached Sharon to say that they were sorry and to talk about other deaths that Bev's had stirred them to remember. The guidance counselors and the school psychiatrist put aside their other work and made themselves available to anyone who wanted to speak to them. Sharon had had her own private session, with all nine of them at once, and it was actually very helpful, she related. In all four grades, English teachers were having their classes write essays about their fears and insecurities. There was a great outpouring of good will going on.

When Terri and I spoke, it was mostly about Sharon. "She seems all right," I said over and over. "How can that be? She loved Bev so much." Terri admitted that she didn't understand herself. I was the one, she said, who she was really worried about. She said that I should consider returning to school.

But I couldn't, because it was my fault. I couldn't bear the thought of seeing Jack in the halls, or any of Bev's other friends. I was the one who had suggested stopping at the diner, even if it was Bev, as Sharon and Terri constantly reminded me, who had summoned us together in the first place. She had been so gloomy, they said; it was almost as if she had known that she was going to her death all along.

Yes, and I had cut her off just as surely as her assailant had, telling my own tale of woe when I knew she had brought us together to tell hers. Terri and Sharon never admitted that that part of the story had been repeated, but I knew it had. Not that I imagined they'd repeated it out of malice. It was simply the truth, a part of a greater truth which was too urgent to be tiptoed around.

Our conversations did little to comfort me, though that didn't stop me from insisting we have them. It amazed me when, after a week or so, Sharon began to suggest that we get off the phone so that she could finish her homework. Terri was kinder; she did her homework while we spoke, which wasn't too difficult a task since I did most of the talking. "Weren't you afraid?" I exclaimed one night well past midnight when Terri mentioned that she had been to the supermarket with her mother. (Except for the funeral, I had not been out of the house at all. And I had let my own mother leave it only once, and that was to get a dead bolt for the front door. Then I sat in the dark holding a Cuisinart blade in my hand like a Frisbee, counting the minutes that it would take her to drive to the store, park, make her purchase, explain to whatever acquaintance that she was bound to run into that she was in a hurry, and drive back home again. And when her actual return preceded the one I had estimated for her by three minutes, I dialed 911 and told them to hold on until I was sure it was her banging on the door, shouting to be let in.)

"I was," Terri said.

"At first I was really afraid. But I looked at every person in every aisle, and I saw that there was no one there who was capable of doing anything like that."

We concluded that part of my problem was that I had never even seen the assailant. By the time they got me out from under the table, a good half hour after the event, he had been covered over with a sheet and was surrounded by police and reporters. Terri and Sharon had seen him come in. They agreed that they had known even before he drew

the gun from his wind-breaker that something was wrong with him. His eyes were glazed over, as if he had just gotten out of bed. And something about the way he held his mouth suggested despair. Terri said it was that his lips were quivering, as if he were cold. There was great pain there, she said; if only I had seen it I would know.

Nor had I seen Bev when the shots were being fired. "Do you think she knew?" I asked my friends anew each evening. Sharon had no idea; she had seen the man and the gun, and then, as she put it, she shut down, lost consciousness without actually fainting. Terri insisted that Bev could have known nothing; she had had her back to the guy, and it had happened too fast, one shot after another. I argued with her on this point, for my experience had been otherwise, but she insisted that Bev hadn't had time to turn around, that she had just begun to say something an instant before the first shot rang out. Terri remembered being surprised to see her lips moving, to learn that her own face revealed no warning of what was to come.

I longed to believe Terri, but being compassionate by nature, I feared she had made her story up for my sake. I hounded Sharon to try and remember. She insisted that although her eyes had witnessed the event, her mind never took it in; she could tell me nothing about it. After some days Terri advised me not to pressure her, to just leave that part of it alone. So we didn't talk about that anymore, and we didn't talk about the brief space of time between that and the arrival of the ambulances. In fact, much of their conversation turned to other matters, things I was missing at school, books that I had better read if I ever wanted to catch up.

There were nights when I took Surge to bed with me, although I knew it cost him something to make the leap. Then I would talk to him, whisper into his big floppy black ear about injustice and fate. "Why Bev?" I asked him a hundred times. "Because she was beautiful? Because she had everything going for her and he had nothing? And what was she going to tell us? What was the secret?" He seemed to listen sympathetically enough, but when I reached for him in the middle of the night as I struggled to free myself from my bleak recurrent dreams, I realized that he had returned to his place on the floor at the foot of my bed.

I was just beginning to think that Terri and Sharon might be extraterrestrials when Terri called one night and said, "We sure started the school year off with a bang, didn't we? I'll tell you one thing, I'll never eat at *that* diner again!" She laughed like a mad woman, not her little hee-hee-hee, but something gruesome and perverse. On and on she went, laughing over my pleas for her to take deep breaths and try to quiet down. When her laughter subsided, she began to sob, deep throaty gasps that I imagined shook her entire body. I stopped talking, mesmerized by the sound of her sobs and the images they evoked.

She was drunk for the second time in her life, the first being the night of the funeral. She had stolen a bottle of gin from her father's liquor cabinet and swallowed down more than a third of it. Her words were so slurred that it took several minutes before she could make me understand what had happened. Sharon had begun private therapy that afternoon, and her therapist had outlined a course of action that was guaranteed to restore her to her former self. Her first recommendation was that Sharon stop spending so much time talking to Terri and me, that she make new friends, pursue new interests. Mrs. Michener was delighted. She'd been telling Sharon for years that she was too gifted a student to be attending public school. They agreed that Sharon would finish up her senior year at the private school in Highland. "So now we've lost them both!" Terri cried into the phone.

We talked for several hours into the night, initially rehearsing what we would say to Sharon to get her to see that the therapist and her mother were wrong, that she needed us more than ever. I said that I couldn't imagine that it would take that much of an effort to turn her around; of the three of us, she had seemed to be coping the best. But then Terri began to sob again, and when she was done, she related some changes in Sharon's behavior; changes, she said, which she hadn't planned to tell me about just yet. Sharon had begun to smoke, not only out in the school yard where it was permitted, but also in the bathrooms, and once she even lit up in the hall. The teachers went easy on her because of what happened. But as soon as they released her, she headed straight for the nearest bathroom and lit up all over again. And while she had always been sloppy, now she had taken it to an extreme. She had worn the same green shirt to school for two weeks straight.

I didn't want to hear it. "She gets attached to things," I interrupted. "Look how long she's been wearing that raincoat of hers."

She'd stopped combing her hair, Terri reported, ignoring my outburst, and she had reason to believe that Sharon wasn't showering either. When I asked her why she had kept all this from me, Terri admitted that she was afraid that if I learned what shape Sharon was in, I'd never come back to school.

She told me other things too. One day in English, for instance, Sharon leaned over to Terri and said, "She set us free in dying. We're immortal now," and when she looked up at her, Terri saw that Sharon was smiling rhapsodically. Then one night Terri arrived at her house unexpectedly, because she had taken one of Sharon's books home by mistake and wanted to return it. She found Sharon writing copiously in a notebook she had never seen before. Sharon covered it up with her arm, but not before Terri saw the word "Corina" written on it; she was *still* working on the play.

"Maybe it was the Faust thing that Bev wanted to talk about," I said. "Maybe she didn't like the idea. Sharon said she was excited about it, but then Sharon was blind where Bev was concerned."

In the end we decided to respect Sharon's decision. We were okay, we told each other, we were getting by. If Sharon wasn't, then she had every right to test the therapist's suggestions. We could only pray that after enough time had passed, she would come back to us. We vowed to stay out of therapy ourselves, to lean on each other when things got tough.

My father had an eerie fascination with the whole business. He came to the house every afternoon during my convalescence and talked to me about it in my room. Had I been myself, I would have realized sooner what he was up to, but as it was, it took a couple of weeks before I began to see that his interest in the assailant, whose name was Thomas Rockwell, was linked to the pirate book that he was working on. His research, he had told me once when he had first begun it, demanded not only that he immerse himself in the times, but also that he come to terms with the nature of evil. And now here he had a shining example—if not of evil, at least of its consequences—right in his own former home. Not that I minded. It was enough to have him in the house, to be able to listen to the brief but civil exchanges that passed between him and Mom as he came and went from my room.

They only argued once, but it was a bad one. He had closed my door behind him, but I opened it a crack and listened to them out in the kitchen. What Mom wanted to know was whether he'd talked to me yet about going into therapy. He admitted that he hadn't. When did he think he'd get around to it? Mom asked. Apparently she'd been hounding him for some days, because there was bitterness in her tone, and Dad, who wasn't big on therapy in the first place, reacted to it by making some crack about Mom's therapist having done her more harm than good. "When the house is already built," he said, "you don't go messing with the foundation." To which Mom replied, "You're threatened, aren't you? You're afraid that your name might come up, that you might have to take some responsibility for her inability to cope."

I closed my door then, but they got louder and I could hear what was said anyway. "Is that what you think?" Dad shouted. "That I would stoop to put my own insecurities before her welfare? Well, I've got news for you. I happen to think she *is* coping. Shutting yourself off for a time is not an inappropriate response to what happened. And I happen to think that a girl as smart as Ginny will reach her own conclusions about how to deal with all this in the long term. *I* trust her judgment!" "And *I* don't?" Mom screamed back.

Since I was unable to do any reading myself at the time, it was Dad who read me the newspaper articles describing Rocky's life and his neighbors' impressions of him. Rocky, who was thirty-two when he died, had worked in a bakery, but he had lost his job some months prior to the killings, not because of anything he had done but because he was low man on the totem pole when a second bakery opened in the same neighborhood and took away half their business. The woman he had worked for was quoted as saying, "He kept to himself, did his work, and went home. The only thing that I could say that was peculiar about him was that he could never remember to punch out his time card, had a blind spot when it came to that."

He lived alone, had never been married, never had any friends over that anyone knew about. He watched a lot of TV, his neighbors at his apartment complex said. He kept the volume up high and they could hear it through the walls at all hours of the night. Until the advent of his unemployment, however, they had only actually seen him coming and going. Then, this past summer, he had spent a lot of time stretched out in a lawn chair down by the pool. When asked about his mood, the other sun-bathers admitted that they had never spoken to him. He always seemed to be asleep or verging on it. "He didn't have much of a life," Dad said.

I might have said the same of him, with his barren kitchen counters. I remembered Goliath then, but she had been swept so far from the forefront of my mind that I was unable to formulate any questions concerning their relationship.

He read me other articles, about the victims. Our waitress, the first one to be shot, had had a life. In addition to her part-time job, she had been taking courses at Farleigh Dickenson and had wanted to go into physical therapy. She had been married and had two small children. The second shot had claimed the life of Martha Gardener, wife of Herman Gardener, mother of Sheila Gardener, whose Thanksgiving dinner would not be the one I had imagined for her. Martha had been a bookkeeper, the organist at their church, a girl scout leader, and a Mensa member. The third shot had taken Bev, whose story my father had the decency to refrain from reading. The fourth did not kill its victim. Michael Brine's shoulder wound would heal and he would eventually return to his wife, child, and his dry-cleaning business. The fifth, of course, Rocky had swallowed.

When each day was done, when I had exhausted my mother, been exhausted by my father, and put down the phone receiver for the night, I thought about Herman Gardener. I thought about the way he had flirted with his wife, and, moments later, the way he had opened his mouth and bobbed his head in defiance of reality. I learned from my father's newspaper articles that he lived in Ridgewood, New Jersey.

Herman Gardener, the man who had helped me to my feet after my fall in front of the diner, helped me out again, this time unwittingly. I had called him once, but when he answered, I lost my nerve and hung up the phone. I decided that it would be better to talk to him in person. But when I asked my mother if I could borrow her car, she said that I appeared to be in no condition to drive and offered to take me wherever it was that I wanted to go. I could no more arrive at Herman Gardener's house with my mother than I could with my father, who also offered to drive me when I asked for his car. So, four weeks after the event, I made up my mind to return to school—if only for the sake of appearances.

4

I was nervous. It had never before occurred to me that anyone at my school might be dangerous, but now I had learned the hard way that people can snap and I did not want to be around them. Furthermore, although I knew from what Terri had told me that the general hysteria had died down, I expected to be surrounded the moment I stepped off the bus by a host of curiosity seekers looking for yet another angle on the story. I had prepared a brisk response, the kind officials offer when they are questioned on issues they haven't yet come to terms with. But either the curiosity of my peers had already been sated or Terri had warned them about what my mother referred to as my "breakdown", because only a few people approached me, and that was only to pat me on the back and welcome my return to school.

My throat was scratchy from a cold that was coming on, and after having talked for four weeks straight and gotten nowhere, I found I didn't even want to talk to Terri. During English, I passed her a note saying that I didn't want to see anybody at lunch, that I felt the need to be alone. She misunderstood and sent a note back saying not to worry, that she had been sitting at our old table over by the trash cans ever since Sharon had left school.

Back in the old days, I might have taken my *Webster's* out of my backpack and copied down the definition of "alone" and passed it back to her. Back in the old days, Terri would have giggled and copied something nasty—the definition of "hard-hearted", say—from her own dictionary. But this wasn't the old days, so we sat in the cafeteria together, nibbling at our sandwiches and nodding at our more jovial classmates when they came our way to dump their trash. The only one who actually stopped at our table was Jack, Bev's boyfriend, or ex, I guess you'd say. For one terrible moment he stared at me. Then he lowered his eyes and nodded like the others and turned to sweep his empty milk carton into the metal can. "Ain't much to say, is there?" Terri whispered.

"How was school?" my mother asked that evening.

"Okay," I said to her back.

She was slamming things around in the cupboard, trying to find the new jar of mustard so that we could get on with our hot dogs. She had just begun to mutter to herself when, happily, she found it. When she turned around, she was smiling. It occurred to me that her well-being hinged these days on the outcome of just such minor challenges. "That's all? Just okay?"

I shrugged. I didn't feel like talking.

"I made up my mind not go to my class tonight," she announced.

I made no comment. She furrowed her brows, staring at me as if she had anticipated a specific response.

"It's not that I think you're still too . . . what? . . . fragile . . . to be left alone. Or that anything's going to happen. I don't want you thinking that. It's just that I've missed so much that I don't think I can make it up."

Until the day at the diner, there were several events that she had attended in the evenings. I had no idea which one she was referring to now. My expression must have reflected my confusion because she said, "Tai Chi; tonight was Tai Chi."

There was some resentment in her tone, but the absence of the smart remark that I would have ordinarily spit back enabled her to hear it for herself. "It's not a big deal," she said, stretching her lips. "He'll be starting a new class in a month. And of course my missing the others, my book club and my support group and bingo, won't set me back at all." She laughed abruptly. "Which isn't saying much for any of them, is it?"

In spite of the fact that I was only smiling, she sang, "Oh, it's good to see you laughing," and got up from the table. She opened up the refrigerator and got out a can of diet

Coke, our drink of choice, popped the tab with her thumb, and refilled both our glasses. "But I did invite someone over tonight," she continued cautiously. "Ida Newet. I hope you don't mind."

Again she furrowed her brows and scrutinized me. I had told her many times that I didn't want anyone over except Dad until I had come to terms with this whole thing. But now I only stared back at her. She bit down on her bottom lip and released it. "She's been asking about you," she said finally. "'How's Ginny? When can I see her?' So I figured it was best to get it over with."

Two things were immediately clear to me: One, Mom was lying about why Ida wanted to come over, and two, Mom felt guilty for saying that she could. Not a very interesting observation, perhaps, but one which, I realized with some surprise, had I not been silent, I might not have gleaned.

Ida and Charles Newet were the only couple from their former lives that my parents had remained friends with. Or, rather, my mother still saw Ida, although infrequently, and my father still saw Charles. Ida ran a day-care center somewhere in town, and Charles had a business machine store that employed some thirty people.

When she knocked, Mom and I had just finished the dishes and were back at the table. I was making an effort to read the newspaper and Mom was having her plastic after-dinner cigarette. I got up before Mom, asked who it was, and unbolted the door. Ida embraced me immediately and whispered "poor baby" into my ear. Then she held me by the shoulders and looked me over. "Well, you look much better than you did at the funeral," she said. I smiled. I didn't even remember her being there.

She sank into a chair at the table, across from where Mom was sitting. She was a short woman, but unlike Mom, who worked out and watched her weight, Ida had let herself go. She wasn't exactly fat, but her ass had spread, and the bulk around her middle had kept her from wearing her blouses tucked in for the last couple of years. Her hair, which was a shiny light brown and very healthy-looking, was her best feature, though she didn't make enough of it. She wore it short, cut just below her ear, and since it was thin, it clung to her round face. The skin of her face—her second best feature—was ivory white and virtually wrinkleless. If not for her weight and her hairstyle—or rather lack of one—and the brown-and-yellow mottled glasses she wore, she might have been youthful-looking. "Oh, Janie," she said. "It's so good to see you."

Mom stretched a hand across the table and patted Ida's. "It's good to see you too."

They both turned to look at me, their thin smiles quivering on their faces. "Homework," I said, and I cocked my head towards the hall.

Back in the old days, I had always done my homework with earphones on. I liked classical, usually Mozart, for English, jazz for social studies and the other subjects where you had to read but not necessarily to form an opinion, and grunge for everything else. It was a habit I had acquired some time ago when my parents had first begun to argue. But as I was hungry for whatever morsel of distraction Mom and Ida might provide me with, I put my Walkman aside and left my door slightly opened. A new thought had come to me during the course of the day, and I marveled that it hadn't occurred to me sooner. Of the four people who had died that day, I had not only spoken to three of them just before their deaths, but I had also been angry with each of the three—Bev and the waitress for their disregard of my needs, and Martha Gardener for being married to the man I had wished had been my father. My anger, it was conceivable, had put a spot on them. And like the bull's-eye drawn on the target-practice figure, it had shown Thomas Rockwell where to aim. I hadn't spoken to or been angry with Michael Brine and he hadn't died. If I had, he might have.

Out in the kitchen I could hear Ida Newet saying, "His eyes are glazed over when I talk to him, Jane. It's like he's not even hearing what I say."

"It's work," my mother offered. "He's under so much pressure there."

"Oh come on, Jane. Don't patronize me. I came to you

for help. Tell me the truth. Was Ed like that, when it was going on?"

Mom laughed. "Ed was always like that, so I can't say."

I opened my notebook and began to review for a math quiz. Luckily, we were still going over stuff we had learned last year, so I hadn't fallen too far behind. The phone rang, twice before I picked it up. "How you doing?" Terri asked. "Not bad," I said. "Have you heard from Sharon?" "Not one word. But I saw her from the bus on the way home. She was with her mother. She was probably driving her to the therapist again. I miss her so much, Ginny. I miss *us* so much. What are we going to do?"

"If you hear from her, let me know," I said. "I can't really talk now. We've got company over."

There was a pause. Then she said, "I understand." There was no indignation in her tone; I believed she did understand.

I did my homework at a snail's pace, for my attention span had dwindled to about two minutes. After that, even if I kept my eyes glued to the page in front of me, I stopped seeing the words and saw instead the images—Herman Gardener helping me to my feet, his hand lifting as if to cover his face, Bev's eyes scrutinizing me over her menu, the waitress waiting for my response, her back, her blouse, her pad and pen, his bobbing head, his slumping wife, Terri's legs, Bev's legs, Bev's chair, Bev dead.

These images did not come and go the way you might expect. Rather, they were always there, had been since the day of their inception, though some of the time I was able to function over them—the way you attend to other matters while the TV is on without losing full awareness of it. Sometimes it was *only* the images, and that was not so bad. Other times the questions followed—everything from *Why Bev?* to *What is the significance of Thomas Rockwell failing to punch out his time card?* A blind spot, his former employer had said. And the thing about the questions was that there were no answers for any of them. In fact, they only generated more questions. I had always envied Sharon and Terri the ability to live so thoroughly in their minds. Be careful of what you ask for, right? I lived in mine now. It was a torture chamber from which there was no escape, a little black room with a solitary window from which I could see out but not squeeze through. "I can't talk to him about it," I heard Ida Newet saying in the kitchen. "I've tried. He's says I'm imagining. He says I'm nagging. I feel . . . I feel . . . so unloved."

"How about some wine?" Mom suggested.

"I can't," Ida said. "He'll want to know why I was gone so long."

"So let him wonder," Mom said.

I finished my homework and got my trampoline out from under the bed and began to jump. Thomas Rockwell wasn't the only crazed individual in recent times who had gone into a public place to take some lives before he took his own. I had read somewhere in a magazine that violence is cyclical. The last period of unfathomable violence in America had occurred in the 1920s. The one before that was the period about which my father was writing. Another coincidence?

The women were laughing in the kitchen. Apparently the wine was doing them some good. "It's my damn bladder," I heard my mother say. "Don't laugh! How do you think it looks at work? There I was, on my way over to the copier . . . and I *knew* he was watching . . . and suddenly I stop walking and sort of squeeze my legs together, sneeze, and go back about my business! Ida, I have to carry extra panties in my bag when I have a cold!"

Ida Newet howled. "Well, at least it's not as blatant as mine," she said. "What do you think my kids think when they're telling me their long-winded stories and suddenly I reach into my bag and pull out my inhaler and stick it up my nose?"

I laughed aloud, for the first time in weeks. I had seen Ida Newet do that once. It gave me a moment's comfort to think that these two middle-aged women could joke about their ailments. I tried to think if I had ever heard men do the same thing. I jumped off my trampoline and kicked the door closed and jumped back on again. No, my father had a bad back and Charles was prone to anxiety attacks, but I had never heard them discuss it together, much less laugh about it. I wondered if this male deficiency was linked to their potential for violence. I wished with all my heart that I could call Sharon—not the new Sharon but the old one, the one I had served, loved, and amused all my life—and ask her. Violent crimes were infrequent where we lived, compared to those that occurred in other places. Yet every time I opened the newspaper, I found more evidence that violence was everywhere, all-prevailing. A woman just a few years older than me had run out into the street naked to avoid being raped the other night. An eleven-year-old girl had watched her mother's boyfriend try to get her head into a noose. A boy a year younger than me had slain his father and his father's girlfriend, disposed of the bodies, and then invited his friends over for a party. When the reporters interviewed his friends, they said he was a good kid, helpful and patient. Had there been some telltale sign, some *blind spot* his friends had missed because they were too preoccupied with their own lives? Or had he really been a good kid all along, right up until that moment when he made the decision?

I jumped off the trampoline, grabbed the TV remote control from my night table, and resumed jumping. Before the killings, I would have clicked until I came to a love story, a rock concert, or, knowing that Sharon would probably be watching it, PBS. Now I had no interest in any of them.

It took only a few seconds until I found a slasher film. A terrified-looking woman, who might have been blind, was feeling her way down a hallway when a door opened behind her, revealing, at first, only a shadow. Then a man with a knife held high over his head stepped out of the shadow. Unlike the description of Thomas Rockwell that I had had from Sharon and Terri, this guy looked utterly calm. If there was supposed to be pain there, the actor was incapable of portraying it.

I clicked again, until I had MTV. A heavy metal band was playing, its lead singer screeching demonically, while a woman in a torn blouse crouched against a brick wall, hugging her shoulders and looking from side to side anxiously. I clicked once more and found a dark-haired girl crouched in the corner of a stairwell with her knees up to her chest, almost like the woman I had just seen. The child was holding her hands on her ears. Two men could be heard shouting, and the louder they got, the more the child's face contorted. Then a door slammed, and a man, presumably one of the shouters, appeared in the frame. "Come on," he said, gently, so that I thought at first he must be okay. Then I realized that the child still seemed terrified, and when he repeated his command, it was more of a growl than anything else.

Were these, I wondered, the types of shows that Rocky had watched? Was this the source from which he had got his courage?

I turned the volume to mute and jumped and listened to the muffled laughter coming from the kitchen. Then I put away the trampoline and turned on my computer. When I was happy with the letter, I printed it and left my room.

Mom and Ida Newet were standing at the door, Ida with her hand on the knob. Her ivory skin had turned pink, just like the Zinfandel they had been drinking. "Oh, it was great to see you again!" she said to me. When she hugged me, it was with a good deal more gusto than she had upon her arrival.

"Well," Mom said after she had gone. "I hope she makes sit home okay."

"Mom, I won't be talking anymore for a while," I said.

"Thank God she doesn't hab ver' far tuh go."

"And I'll need you to make several copies of this letter for me."

She took it from my hand, widening her eyes three or four times to get them to focus. "To who mit mi' concern," she read aloud.

She must have heard how she sounded because she read the rest to herself—more than once if the time she took was any indication. Then she put the letter on the table, where we both stared at it for some moments. "Yer not goin' to to . . . to talk anymore?" she asked softly.

It seemed as good a time as any to start, so I pointed to "temporarily" in the second paragraph of my letter. She looked at me. She was so woozy she had to grab the back of the chair to keep her balance. "How many c-copies dyuh want?"

I held up my hands and spread my fingers. "Ten?" she

asked. I made fists and then spread them again. "Tuh-wenty, th-thirty, f-forty, fi-fifty," she counted. I made an X with my pointers and then held them apart. She nodded. "Fi-fifty times two. One hunred copies," she said. "I got it. I'll do it. After all, I trus' yer judgment."

5

Ida Newet became a regular at our house, as did the Zinfandel my mother stocked for her visits. Sometimes she would come right from work, and then she and Mom would share the same glass, like sisters, I thought, before Ida hurried home to cook for Charles and my mother ran off to her evening activities. Other times, when Charles had to work late and Mom had a free night, the two would shop or take in a movie, and then Ida would come back for a couple of glasses before she went home. Most of the time they talked about Charles, or the twins, who were both away at different colleges in Boston. Other times they talked about me. "I think it's okay," I heard Mom say one night. "I trust her judgment. I really do. I think her silence is a sign that she's angry, that she's outraged. As well she should be. She was a victim too. Everyone who was in the diner that day was. The shooting was random. I think she's searching for the right voice to communicate that."

Mom's words of wisdom must have meant something to Ida personally, because one Saturday morning in late October when Mom was on the phone with her, I heard Mom say, "You what? You found your voice? What do you mean?"

I tiptoed to my door to hear better, but when I peeked out, I saw Mom coming down the hall. I emerged so as not to appear to have been eavesdropping. "Ida's on the phone," Mom said. "She wants to know if we want to picnic with her today up on the mountain."

The invitation was not an aberration. Ever since I'd stopped talking, Mom and Ida always tried to include me in their excursions, all of which I declined. It was not that they wanted my company as much as it was that they wished to

offset the invitations they believed I no longer received from
Sharon and Terri. But I was not quite the outcast they imagined. To the contrary, once I had distributed my letters at
school and given their recipients a day or two to digest them,
I took my place in the cafeteria with the very same group of
kids I had been sitting among since the middle of the year
before—which is to say, Bev's friends. I listened to all of their
conversations—few of which had to do with Bev anymore—
and if I had some input, I wrote it on the pad I always carried
now and slid it down the table to the person for whom my
remark was intended. Sure, there were some rolled eyes,
some crusty comments, but for the most part, my acquaintances indulged me. When a party or some other social event
was planned, I was invited along with everyone else—whether
out of pity, or for Bev's sake, or because now that I was suffi-
ciently flawed I was more genuinely liked, I really couldn't
say—even after it became clear that I wouldn't accept. See, it
wasn't that I craved company—you don't when you live in
your mind. But the alternative to sitting with them was to sit
with Terri, who knew what was in my mind and might have
wanted to talk about it. My mother and Ida Newet, however,
didn't know about my invitations because no one ever called
me on the phone. You can communicate with a non-talker
in person, but you can't telephone her.

I nodded affirmatively and saw a flicker of surprise flash
in Mom's eyes. She went back down the hall. "Yes, she'll come
too," she said too cheerfully to be sincere.

Except for school, where I now felt reasonably safe, I
hadn't been out in public since the killings. The familiarity
of the landscape nearly made me gasp. I stayed low in my
seat in Mom's Yugo and kept an eye out for hostile faces in
the few cars we passed on our way up the mountain. Surge,
whose company I had insisted on, was in the back seat, which
was barely big enough to contain him.

Ida was standing beside her Four-Runner when we pulled
into the lot. As soon as she saw us, she began to bob up and
down on her little feet and to flutter her hand in the air.
Sitting on her hood was one of those huge, old-fashioned

47

straw picnic baskets with hinges in the middle of the wooden cover. A loaf of Italian bread was protruding from one end. "What a day!" Ida cried as we got out. "Look at the sky! Look at the valley! Look at the trees!"

We looked up, down, and ahead, as directed. Then, as if she thought I might be deaf as well as dumb, Ida stepped right in front of me. "I have a special place," she said breathlessly. "It's back a ways. There won't be many people there, if any. But I wanted to ask you first. Do you think you'd be more comfortable with other picnickers around?"

Frankly, neither had much appeal. I had come along only because the thought of driving down to Herman Gardener's house in Ridgewood, New Jersey, was becoming increasingly more frightening as time went by. Before I could attempt it, I would have to get used to getting out locally. I threw out my hands as if to say, "Whatever." Ida caught one on the decline and gave it a little squeeze. Then she took up her basket and signaled for us to follow.

We might have been three of the seven dwarves, hi-hoing our way along the forest path. Happy hummed and swung her basket. Grumpy, who wasn't much for the outdoors, turned her head from side to side, recoiling from the foliage where it protruded and running down a list of all the people she knew with Lyme disease. I suppose I was Dopey, because as soon as the analogy occurred to me, I began to wonder in earnest when we would encounter our antagonist.

But we encountered no one, and by the time we had arrived in the birch forest, I was enjoying the scenery and the crisp air almost as much as Ida was. The trees were all young, slender, healthy, and about the same height—which is to say dwarfish, like Mom and Ida and me. Their leaves flickered in the breeze like gold coins. We found a small clearing, and Ida set about spreading out the contents of her basket on the red-and-white checkered tablecloth she had brought. She cut off the crusty ends of the bread and fed them to Surge. Then she divided the rest of the loaf into three sections.

She had thought of everything. In addition to a wide variety of cold cuts, she had potato salad, macaroni salad, and cole slaw in Tupperware containers. There was mustard, mayonnaise, Italian dressing, and dill pickles and chips, as well as apples, pears, and cupcakes for dessert. "You've got more here than we have in our whole kitchen at home," Mom said sadly. "No wonder he's the way he is. You're too good to him. Take it from me, it doesn't pay."

"Him" was Charles. They spoke of him so often that it was no longer necessary to say his name. But they seldom spoke of him in front of me, which was probably why they both glanced at me just then.

I put my sandwich together hurriedly and turned aside, so that my back was to them. I rolled my head around on my shoulders, so that it would seem that my interest was in the scenery. They spoke for some moments about work, Mom's and Ida's, and then Ida described the dress that she had decided to wear to some function that she would be attending with Charles. Then, no longer able to restrain herself, Mom said, "So, tell me. What's this about your voice?"

Ida chose her words carefully. "Well, Jane, I got to thinking about some of the things you've said recently, and I decided that you were right. Each of us has to have a way of saying how we feel about ourselves. And sometimes words aren't enough. You talk and talk and talk, and nobody listens anyway." She stopped to see whether I would turn around. I didn't. "Well," she went on. Then she sighed abruptly. "Well, look."

There was a moment of silence, so that at first I thought they might be using hand-signals. Then Mom exclaimed, "Oh my God!" and Ida tapped me on the shoulder.

When I turned, she was twisting her head away from me and holding her thin hair up on one side of her head. "I love it!" Mom cried. "I think it's great. I absolutely love it!"

I couldn't see anything. Mom discerned that I was puzzled and told me to come closer. And there, in the little clearing between the back of her ear and her hairline was a red tattooed heart with a fancy gold "I" in its center.

"I think it's wonderful," Mom reiterated. "I love it, I just love it." But it was me that Ida was watching for a response. I took my little notebook from my pocket and wrote, *Why the "I"? Or is it supposed to be a "one"?*

"It's an I," Ida said. We blinked at each other. "An I for Ida. It's perfect, you see, because no one will ever know it's there unless I show it to them." She laughed. "Or unless I stand on my head. But *I* know it's there."

"It must have hurt like hell," Mom interrupted.

"Oh, yeah, it did. I had such a headache when I left. And I had to sit holding my ear bent over so that the woman could work on it. All I could think of was, what if my ear stays like this?"

I still don't understand, I scribbled, pushing my pad between their faces.

Ida spread her fingers out and her mouth opened as if she were groping for the words. "Well, Ginny, it's like this," she said finally. "I haven't been feeling too good about myself lately." She glanced at Mom. "With the twins gone off to college and all . . . It's kind of lonely. Separation anxiety or something, I guess. It's hard to explain. It's just that I've been thinking of myself as this little, fat, useless, middle-aged woman—"

"Oh, come on, Ida. You're not fat *or* useless," Mom interrupted again.

This time Ida's eyes didn't stray. She was rolling now, saying this as much for her own benefit as for mine.

"—but your mother and I have had some talks," she continued, her fingers fluttering. "And I've come to realize that I'm more than this little, fat, useless, middle-aged woman. There are things about myself that I like. Lots of things—though I forget that sometimes. So I got the tattoo." She looked upward, at a hawk that was circling overhead. "I got the tattoo so that I would remember to love myself." And then, without any warning, she burst into tears.

I liked Ida Newet's tattoo, when all was said and done. Or rather, I liked the idea that she had changed something about her outward appearance in the hope that it would generate some change within. The weird kids at school, the ones who had blue hair, mohawks, or earrings in their noses, I had always thought of as show-offs, but now I saw that they were only trying to do the same thing as Ida, to muster up a voice that was more than a voice—although Ida's was a whisper by comparison. I stood half the night in front of the mirror playing with my hair, pushing it up over my head and trying to see what it would look like spiked. I pulled it back, to see how I would look with it shaved, and then got out some of Mom's scarves to see how I looked in different colors. I tried to imagine going over to Dad's with a flamingo pink crew cut. Would he smile his noncommittal smile then, I wondered?

I hadn't been over to his place in weeks. He was still coming to visit me, but not as regularly as before. Unlike my mother and the kids at school, he seemed uncomfortable with my not talking, probably because he wasn't much of a talker himself. When they lived together, even before the first computer, Mom used to tell him that he was boring.

I need the car, I wrote on my pad a few evenings later, and I went to find Mom. She had just returned from her support group meeting and was sitting on the floor in the living room near the stereo, listening to an old Mamas and Papas album. She had the volume turned down low, but when she saw me coming, she lowered it even more, as if her choice revealed some secret she didn't want to let me in on.

She looked at my pad and handed it back to me. "It's dark," she whispered. "Where could you possibly want to go?"

I had left my pen in my room, so I crossed my arms over my chest, stretched my lips, and set my eyes at half-mast, nodding the way my father used to when she was running at the mouth about something he couldn't care less about. I thought it would make her laugh, but she only said, "To Daddy's?" in a voice that was an octave higher than her usual one.

She looked aside, as if for some excuse. "This is a school night. You won't be fresh for the morning."

I made a face. She had seen my tests. I was doing fine at school, better than ever. Only my English teacher had been concerned that my grades would fall if I continued to refuse to participate in class. But I compensated by handing in two research papers when only one was due, and she hadn't said a word to me about it since.

She made an attempt at a smile. "You haven't driven since . . . well, you know."

I held up four fingers.

"I know it's only four miles. But it's dark and the roads are wet and . . ."

I rolled my eyes. I knew it was dark. No one knew better than I did how dark it was.

"Okay," she said, sighing, and she looked down at her lap. I could see that her support group hadn't done her much good tonight.

I followed her into the kitchen and watched while she rummaged for the keys in her purse. I had my jacket on and was on my way out the door when she cried, "Wait!"

She bit down on her lip and stared at me for a moment and then turned toward the refrigerator. After another moment spent considering it, she stood on her toes and took down a tin of cookies from on top. She sighed. "Here," she said, almost angrily, pushing the tin at me. "Give these to him." She shrugged. "We've had them a week and we haven't touched them. They'll just get stale."

We looked at each other. She seemed to be defying me to interpret her gesture for what it really was. One smile, I knew, one hint that I was overjoyed, and she would snatch her offering back. I whistled, and Surge came lumbering in from the living room. "You can't take him there," Mom said flatly. His expression seemed to convey the same message. I rolled my eyes at the both of them and went out the door. "Watch for deer," my mother called out behind me.

Right.

I had already prepared my father's note. It was in my bag with the cookie tin. It read: *I have decided to spike my hair and dye it purple. I refuse to be a victim. This will be my way of saying that I have power over my life, my fate.*

Until that moment I couldn't have said why I was giving him advance notice, except that I had contemplated my arrival at his door with purple hair for the last two nights, and I kept coming up blank when I tried to imagine his reaction. I thought I knew how he would react to the note, however. He would tell me to sit down so that we could talk about it. Maybe he would even see that hidden between the lines was the message that he had victimized me too. Maybe we would talk about that. My mother was ready to forgive him. Why else would she have given me the cookies? If they hadn't been on top of the refrigerator where I couldn't reach them, they'd have been gone by now. She had bought them for him in the first place. It was time to clear the air. If he gave me some assurance that he was coming back soon, I'd let him talk me out of the new do.

Driving the dark country roads was more unsettling than I had anticipated. The prospect of my parents verging on a reconciliation only added fuel to my anxiety. Every time I went around a bend I expected my headlights to reveal a man with dazed eyes and a quivering mouth stepping out from under the trees, drawing his weapon from inside his wind-breaker. If I were shot down now, Mom's message would go undelivered, her moment of recklessness forever forgotten in the midst of the chaos that would surely follow. If I'd had another car, I would have accelerated, so as to be prepared to run him down before he could take aim. The Yugo, I imagined, could be stopped with a foot, even an extended arm.

I almost knocked; that was how threatened I still felt from my last visit. But the lights were low, and there was no noise coming from inside. Besides, it was dark out there, and eerily quiet. I was a sitting duck as long as I hesitated.

I turned the knob quietly and entered. He wasn't in the kitchen. His computer was off, and except for an empty wine bottle, the area around it was clear. I walked into the living room and gaped at the three surprised faces I found there, my father's, Charles Newet's, and Goliath's. Goliath's hand was on her heart. "Ginny!" my father said, rising. "We thought it was a burglar!"

Charles Newet got up too. "Ginny, Ginny, Ginny," he cried, so that I had no opportunity to study my father's expression for signs of disappointment.

Charles had an oblong face to begin with, but with his black hair receding at his forehead and his head tucked back so that his chin was doubled, it seemed much longer than the last time I had seen him, several months ago. He waddled towards me, his arms outstretched, his feet pointing outward too, like a duck's. "I'm so sorry about your friend," he whispered as he embraced me.

When he stepped away, I found Goliath towering before me with her hand out. "I'm Rita Drabble," she said. She was pretty, I noted with displeasure, much prettier than I had realized that night out on the catwalk. She looked about ten years younger than my father, and roughly the same height.

I must have lifted my hand automatically, because the next thing I knew she was shaking it firmly. "You don't have to tell me who you are," she exclaimed. "I know all about you. I'm so glad to meet you, Ginny."

Once the formalities were concluded, they all stood staring at me, and I was tempted to say something just to dispel the awkwardness. Then I remembered the cookies and removed them from my bag and put them down on the coffee table, between Rita and Charles's wine glasses. I didn't intend to bang the tin, but when I saw my father cringe, I realized that I had. I took my notebook out and scribbled, *From Mom* on a blank page and ripped it off, putting it on top of the tin where everyone could see it. My father just stared at me, his lips stretched and his blue eyes twinkling, while Rita and Charles bent to read the note together in the dim light. Then Rita removed it and opened the tin. "Tell your mother thank you," she said. She laughed. "Ed never has anything worth eating here. A woman could starve to death."

I recovered from my moment of cowardice and quickly scribbled, *You don't look like you're starving to me,* and handed it to her. She laughed again, this time throwing her head back so that her long, reddish hair fell behind her shoulders. "I like a kid with a sense of humor," she said. I stared at her in disbelief. "Well sit down," she said. "Have some cookies. Ed, get your daughter a glass of milk." When my father had turned, she added loudly, "And me too!" Then she looked at Charles. "You?" she asked. He smiled and shook his head. "You can't eat cookies with wine, Charles," she whispered.

I sat on the floor, on the other side of the coffee table, and watched her pick through the tin. She lifted one of the little accordion wrappers and grunted with pleasure when she realized that there was another layer beneath it. Then one by one she lifted each of the others, her brows rising when she came upon varieties she hadn't expected. I glanced at Charles Newet, and he smiled and cocked his head as if to say, "Look, she's forgotten that we're here."

Finally she slid the tin out of her way, leaning forward and setting her elbows down on her long legs and her chin down on her knuckles. The neckline of her tie-dyed T-shirt was so loose that I could see the rise of her large breasts beneath it. "Your father was just telling us about his book," she said. "Anne Bonny and Mary Read. Fascinating story. I had never heard of them myself." She threw her head back and snorted at the ceiling. "I didn't even know there *were* female pirates! I think it's great. I believe that women should have adventures just like men do. That's the problem, you know. Girls your age aren't given the freedom that boys are. Because men are predators and women are generally their prey. But it doesn't have to be that way. Why, when I was a kid—"

My father appeared, empty-handed. "We don't have any milk," he confessed.

"So where were you all this time?" Goliath cried.

My father displayed his palms, as if to indicate that he didn't know where he had been.

6

I wrote it all down, every bit of it (not in my little conversational pad but on several sheets of loose-leaf paper from the back of one of my notebooks), and handed it to Terri first thing in the morning, when we passed each other in the hall on the way to our respective homerooms.

I arrived at English with a few moments to spare. And so certain was I that she would have read my narrative by then and would want to comment on it that I waited for her out in the hall. When she didn't show up, I peeked into the classroom, and there she was, her head deep in her text. Then the bell rang, so that I had no chance to confer with her; and after class, she was up and out the door before I had even gathered up all my books.

At lunch I went to her table, over by the trash cans. I had gone there on several occasions over the weeks, to ask if she wanted to join us at the table where I ate—not that I thought she would or should. Always her answer was the same: she had some reading to do; she wanted to be alone. *Can I sit?* I wrote on my lunch bag, and since she had not yet acknowledged my appearance, I dangled the bag before her face.

She looked from my message to her lunch—a half a ham sandwich and a bowl of lettuce in a plastic container—to the book that she had opened up beside it. Heather, one of the girls I usually ate with, motioned to me from across the room. I shook my head and she made a face. "Go ahead, sit," Terri said, finally, "though I don't know what you want me to say, other than that I'm sorry for you. I suppose that's what you want to hear."

What I wanted to hear was anything that she might say. I had written down the events of the last few days as much for her sake as for my own. Ida's tattoo and my meeting with Goliath were, by comparison with what was usually on my mind, mundane matters to be sure, but that was precisely the point. Envisioning the conversation that Terri and I might have (yes, I planned to talk when the time was right) had distracted me from the TV screen that was my mind for half hours at a time. The night before I had dreamed not of the diner, the blouse, the bobbing head, the legs, the chair . . . , but of Goliath. In my dream, she was in our kitchen, rummaging through the refrigerator. Apparently unaware that I was standing just behind her, she took out a carton of eggs and opened it up on the counter. She counted them aloud, and then turned abruptly.

So what, that she threw one at me? So what, that I was unable to scream? In another time it might have been a nightmare. By my new standards, it was a cause for celebration. I wanted to tell Terri that a return to normalcy was at hand. I wanted to share it with her. More than anything, I wanted to hear her refreshing hee-hee-hee again.

She had spread her napkin on her lap, and now she set about unwrapping her sandwich and removing the lid from the salad container. "Bev was right in a way," she said. "It's not your business. They're separated. He has a right to have a girlfriend if he wants to. I agree that he should have told you. He should have told you weeks ago."

Aimlessly, she moved the lettuce leaves around with her fork. Then she sighed and looked at me directly for the first time. When I saw how red and swollen her eyes were, I began to understand why she had been avoiding me all morning. She had been drinking again, I guessed, maybe regularly. She needed saving, but my description of my dream (which I had included in my written narrative), I realized with disappointment, would not do the job.

"As far as your hair goes," she went on almost heatedly, "I think that's ridiculous. What is purple hair going to prove? That you can shock people? Come on, Ginny. They talk about you now, behind your back, as I'm sure they do me. Nothing mean, they just think that your response to what happened— this not-talking thing—is out of proportion to what happened itself. Bev was *their* friend they say; *you* hardly knew her. And here they're getting on with their lives. They don't see why it should be all that different for us just because we happened to be there at the time. If you come into school with purple hair, they'll abandon you altogether. I'm not saying this to be mean. I just don't want to see you make a fool of yourself. I think your mother's friend had the right idea. If you've got to have some symbol for the power you feel you possess, then keep it to yourself. Tattoo a dinosaur on your ass. Or pin amulets to your underwear. But you know what? It won't do a bit of good anyway, Ginny." She removed her glasses and leaned so far over the table that I could see in her eye the reflection of the black hole that was my gaping mouth. "A symbol is only a symbol. You don't have any more power over your life than I do. There's *nothing* that you can do to yourself that will insure that something like that will never happen again."

She glared at me a moment longer. Then she put her glasses back on, slid her book closer, and immediately feigned absorption.

I closed my mouth: she was right, at least where my hair was concerned. I could wear a headdress made of peacock feathers, and I would still be a little, skinny girl, one who looked like an eighth-grader. Sure, I was strong for my size, and I could run fast too, but what were strength and speed compared to a knife, a gun, the fist of a full-grown man empowered by his own derangement?

I watched her read and eat for awhile, and then I reached into my own lunch bag and pulled out the black cat Pez dispenser that Mom had packed for me. I held it out over Terri's book to let her know that I wasn't angry with her in spite of her harsh words. She only nodded as if to say, "Yeah, so what?" Yesterday it had been waxed lips, and the day before that, a little tin racing car with the number "23" painted on its roof. Mom had never even packed my lunches before. Ever since my father left, at which time Mom decided that we could no longer afford hot lunches for me, I had always done that myself. I imagined that the little gifts had been suggested by her therapist, extravagances to stir my curiosity, enticements to lead me to the woman's couch.

I popped a Pez into my mouth and then removed a peanut

butter and jelly sandwich and the orange that I'd seen the day before rolling back and forth in an otherwise empty fruit bin. I hated peanut butter and jelly. If Mom had money to burn, she should have spent it on cold cuts, like Ida Newet did, not on toys from the register counter at the pharmacy. I put the sandwich aside and began to peel the orange. It was thick-skinned, and I could only remove small pieces of the rind at a time. I wished she'd thought to pack a knife.

Terri finished eating and tossed her lunch bag into the trash can. She set her salad container, which was still half full, on top of her book and stood up. "I'm going," she said. She adjusted her glasses. "You really made a mess of it," she added.

I nodded solemnly, because at first I thought she meant my life. When I looked where she was looking though, I realized that she was only referring to my orange. Some of the fruit had come off with the rind and there was juice all over the napkin I had placed beneath it. My hands were sticky, and white fiber threads were hanging from my fingernails. As of yet, I had still not taken a single bite.

"Oh, by the way," Terri said.

I looked up at her; I hadn't realized that she was still standing there.

"I heard from Sharon."

We stared at each other for a moment, I eagerly awaiting an elaboration and she, apparently, considering whether or not she would grant me one. Then she opened the text she had been reading and removed a folded piece of paper from between its pages and handed it to me. "This came in the mail from her. There was no letter, no note, nothing. I wouldn't even have known it was from her if not for the return address on the envelope."

She took her glasses off, wiped them on the bottom of her T-shirt, and replaced them. "Well, maybe I would have known, actually. I guess she's back to her investigations again. Anyway, you can keep it. I copied it for you. I have the original."

I unfolded the paper carefully, so as not to get juice stains on it, and rubbed my fist over its creases several times so that it would lie flat. It was typewritten, single-spaced. At the top,

in caps, it read: *EXCERPT FROM STATEMENT GIVEN BY RAPE VICTIM LOIS MARSH (AGE THIRTY-ONE) TO PO-LICE DURING HER STAY AT BERYL HOSPITAL, WASH-BURN, MISSOURI.*
 I looked up and found that Terri had gone. The cafeteria was beginning to empty. There were a few more minutes to go before the bell that would summon the late-lunchers into the cafeteria and me to study hall. I began to read.
 The plates on my old car, a Toyota pickup, were commercial plates, so they couldn't put them on the new car—because that was a regular car and they said I couldn't use commercial plates. So, I went to Motor Vehicles to return them. It took about twenty minutes, I guess. And when I went back out to the parking lot, I noticed this man pulling in. As I was getting in my car, he was getting out of his. And I probably wouldn't have even noticed him except that he looked at me, stared, you know. He was tall, with dark brows. I don't remember his hair. He might have been wearing a hat. What I noticed, mostly, was his coat. It was this fur job, but the fur was flat, as if it had been ironed. It struck me as strange.
 I had groceries to get, so I pulled out of the lot and went directly across the highway to the supermarket and parked in the lot there. And just as I'm getting out, I see this guy parking again, a few cars away from me. He's not looking at me or anything, but still it seems funny that he pulled up in front of Motor Vehicles, got out, and then got back in again—because he must have pulled out right behind me. So then why did he park in front of Motor Vehicles in the first place? Right?
 So I go into the supermarket, and I take my sweet time, because now I'm thinking, What if he followed me? Not that I really believed it, because why should he have followed me? I mean, why me? But I take my time nonetheless, you know, just in case. And when I come out with my cart, I'm keeping an eye out, just in case. I can't even say what kind of a car he was driving—something oldish, you know, long, like they used to make back then. And I don't see any men sitting in any cars near where I parked, so I stop worrying. I put my groceries in my trunk, push the cart back, and then go into the pharmacy, because I called in a prescription earlier. I get them, the pills, and go back out—and I'm thinking, well, there's no one around. If he did follow me for some perverse reason, he didn't have the patience to wait very long. And I'm just unlocking my door when

I realize that my receipt is lying there on the passenger seat, the one they gave me at Motor Vehicles when I handed in my plates, face up, with my name and address on it. The bell rang and I nearly jumped out of my seat. For a moment I couldn't move. Then I collected my wits and folded up Sharon's paper and stuck it into my shoulder bag. The next step was to wrap up my orange, stick it and the uneaten sandwich and the Pez dispenser back into my lunch bag, toss the works into the trash can, and move on to study hall. But I only sat there, motionless, watching the late-lunchers file in.

A group of freshman girls came in and assembled at one of the tables near the windows. They were all giggles and short skirts, cheerleader types, so pleased to have made it to the high school. They spoke loud, talking more for the benefit of the jocks at the table behind them than to one another, their eyes flashing in their curly-haired heads.

I began to pick at my orange again. The preppies came in, and then the dorks. The headbangers appeared with their long hair hanging in their faces and sat at what had been Bev's table—though of course no one called it that anymore. They too were loud, and because most of their vocabulary came from *Beavis and Butt-head,* obnoxious as well. The bad boys marched in, the troublemakers that every school has, in their combat boots. I must have been sitting at their table because they stopped cold when they saw me there. Then they put their heads together and made a decision, flocking to the table in front of mine. Three of the group were seniors, and one of them was, in spite of his roguishness, in all my honors classes. The word was that Tom Heely sold drugs.

He had just opened his mouth wide enough to receive most of his hamburger when he saw me staring at him. He paused for a moment, his eyes twinkling with amusement. Putting his burger down and keeping his eyes on me, he said something to Frankie Stewart, the junior who was his side kick. Frankie looked around, glanced at me disinterestedly, and went back to his lunch. Tom said something else, about me being the one who had stopped talking, I imagined, and a few of the boys who had their backs to me turned to take a look.

Tom wore two earrings in his left ear and a huge crucifix

around his neck. He had shaved his head at the beginning of the school year, and now his dark hair was just beginning to grow back in. His nose was too big for his face, and there was a jagged scar just above his Adam's apple. He had cut off the sleeves of the black Slayer T-shirt that he wore, and his serpent tattoo was in full evidence. Back in the days before my mother's chief concern had been herself, she had served on the PTA with Tom's mother. A lovely woman, she had said, completely devoted to her five children.

We continued to stare at each other, he smiling and me without expression, I guessed; I was thinking too hard about Sharon's communication, if you could call it that, and about what Goliath had said about men being predators, about it not having to be that way. Frankie, who was the only one of the group who had a brown bag instead of a tray, finished his sandwich and pulled an apple out of his bag. He showed it to Tom, who in turn reached in his pocket and fished out a pocket knife. He thumbed the blade, grinned in my direction, and handed it to Frankie. Frankie peeled his apple and wiped the blade on his jacket sleeve before handing it back.

I lifted a hand and curled a finger. Tom sat there for a moment, squinting. Then, with the rest of them watching, he got up, came around to my table, and sat down across from me. My fingers were trembling and it took a minute to uncap my pen. *Can I borrow your knife?* I wrote on my juice-stained napkin. It tore all around the orange as I turned it.

His teeth flashed. He turned back to look at his friends, but they had already lost interest and were now engrossed in a whispered conversation. "They've got knives up there," he said, and he indicated the front of the cafeteria where the kitchen workers were just cleaning up. I wrote *Plastic butter knives* on what was left of my napkin.

Still grinning at me, he slipped his hand in his pocket and got out his knife. My hands were still quaking, and it became clear right away that I wouldn't get the thing opened. Tom put his palm out. I handed the knife back to him and he opened it for me. I was about to reach for it when he tossed it up in the air and caught it by the blade. Then he handed it back to me handle first. While I was cutting the orange into sections he said, "You want to go out some time? I've never been out with a girl who didn't talk before. It might be interesting."

"No," I said. It was the first word I had spoken in weeks.

7

I had to have money; that was first. But if it was tough looking for a job before, it would be even tougher now that I had taken a vow of virtual silence. I typed up some form letters and passed them around to some of my teachers offering to grade papers, type up handouts, or help them with any outside research they might be involved in. They all responded in kind; they didn't need any help with paper grading or handouts, and none was involved with any outside research.

We had off that Friday for a teachers' convention, and I got Mom to say that I could drive her to work and then keep the Yugo for the day. I waited until noon to drive to my father's, my reasoning being that a Thursday night guest would be long gone by then and a Friday night guest not yet arrived. I burst in as usual, as was my birthright, and slammed my note down on the counter where he was putting a sandwich together. *I need money,* it read. *A lot of it. I don't expect you to just give it to me, especially now that you're dating. But I thought maybe I could do some research for you, help you with your book.*

He either missed the sarcasm or pretended to, but he said that he thought he might be able to use my help. The research, he said, was pretty much done; he knew what he needed to know. But he would love to have me read some chapters, advise him of any weaknesses I came across—as soon as he had a little more done. He could pay me something to do that.

While he was talking, I glanced at his computer and saw that he had been playing solitaire. He noticed and sighed. Then he asked me to sit down, for a soda this time, and a sandwich if I hadn't eaten yet. *Can't,* I wrote. *Too busy. Let me know when you're ready for my services.*

"Wait," he cried as I opened the door, but it was my turn to pretend, and I kept going.

I pulled over in front of the supermarket in town and debated whether to go on looking for work or to drive down to New Jersey, to Herman Gardener's house. In the end, I simply could not imagine myself driving through that much traffic. That would come later, when I had acquired my symbol that was more than a symbol, when I felt safe again.

I forced myself to get out of the car and walked up to the flower shop. I handed the woman there one of the notes that I had prepared. It was succinct. It said only that I was looking for employment, that as I didn't talk, I couldn't consider anything which necessitated verbal skills, but that my other skills more than made up for my deficiency. Stapled to the back of it was proof, a copy of my grades from last year.

The woman's lips quivered. I could see that she didn't know what to make of me. She looked behind her, where a younger woman was arranging bouquets at a table, with her back to us. "We really don't need anyone right now," she said at last. "But come Christmas . . ."

Give me a call then, I wrote, and I left.

I walked up the street, bypassing offices and the stores where I knew communication was all-important. I stopped in at the cleaner's, but the woman there only shook her head. In the glass of each shop I passed, I searched, not for my reflection, but for the reflection of anyone standing behind me, across the street maybe, standing and staring. I smiled at the women and children I passed, because I was both, and I knew where they were coming from. But I dodged the men, even the suits who were coming back from lunch, in fact especially the suits. I was reading the newspaper carefully these days, trying to discern the one peculiarity all assailants had in common. My research confirmed that what was peculiar was that they had none, that seventy-five percent of them appeared to be normal right up until they weren't anymore.

I went into the diner, a smaller, quainter version of the one that Bev had died in, and forced my legs to carry me across the floor. The man at the counter read my note and then took it to someone in the back, in the kitchen, where I hoped they'd let me work. While I waited, I looked over the patrons, watching for sudden movements among them. "Sorry," the man said when he returned.

I ran past the local bar, and faster yet when I saw emerging from it a man with one hand in his pocket. I ducked into the health food store, but when I saw how small it was inside, I ducked out again. I was about to go into the bakery when I remembered with a shock that Thomas Rockwell had worked in one. Defeated, I hurried back down the other side of street, pulling my jacket hood over my head when I had to pass the used-car lot. I was just about to climb into the Yugo and hightail it for the relative safety of home when I saw Ida Newet coming out of the pharmacy with a large brown paper bag. I propelled my hand into the air and waved maniacally until she noticed me.

"Look what I got for my kids," she declared as she approached.

When she was close enough, I peered down into the bag, but I was too distraught to discern more than an array of bright colors. She noticed my face then. "What's wrong?" she asked. "Are you okay? Did something happen?"

I took out a copy of my note and let her read it. Then I shook my head to indicate that my efforts had been unsuccessful. "Oh, poor Ginny," she said. "You could have any one of a dozen jobs if you would just start talking again. Why, I bet I could get Charles to hire you if you'd only agree to use the phone."

I shook my head again. I had gone that route. Being a non-talker agreed with me. I was a listener now. I was listening for danger. It was out there, I could practically smell it. Bev had been sitting across from me. If she had been more aware, had caught the horror reflected in Terri's expression or the significance of Sharon's sudden stupor, she might have ducked while I was still watching Herman Gardener's head bob. Sometimes, late at night, I believed she had known, but hadn't cared, that she had sat erect and willing to accept the fate that might otherwise have been mine. Sometimes, I believed that it was her way of punishing me for telling my story first, that she had decided to take hers with her to the place where such matters are no longer a concern, to leave me voiceless in her place, to let me see how it feels when the thing inside you must go undeclared.

Ida placed a finger over her parted lips and looked aside. "If only . . ." she began. Then, "The budget, the damn budget." Then her finger fell decisively. "My car's over there, next to that black pickup. Do you see it?"

I nodded.

"Do you know the church on Cherry Hill? Of course you do. It's on the way back to your house. Follow me there. I think I might be able to do something for you."

It occurred to me that she might have had a moment of insight, that she knew what was in my mind and was determined to take me up before the altar where we would pray together for the salvation of my soul. But before I could dig my pad out of my pocket and register a complaint, she had turned away and was hurrying through the aisles of parked cars toward her Four-Runner. Then I remembered that I had never heard her talk about religion, and that in all their conversations about "him," neither my mother nor Ida had ever suggested prayer as a possible solution.

We pulled into the lot, which was empty except for two other cars, and she waved me to park alongside her. I parked, but stayed in the car with the motor running. I removed my pen from behind my ear and took a bank receipt from the dash to write on. When I saw her coming towards me, I rolled the window down and held up a finger to indicate that she was to wait a moment. *I'm not Catholic,* I wrote.

She laughed and yanked my door open. "I work here," she said. "This is where the day-care center is."

I looked at the long narrow wing built onto the right side of the church. Oh, I almost said.

We entered a dimly lit hall, with several closed doors along either side of it. Ida opened one. "Go on in and sit down," she said. "I'll be back in a jiffy."

I sat down at the small conference table and looked around. I heard the muffled voices of children, at some distance, below me in the basement, I thought. The floor I was on was completely silent. I wondered about the other cars in the lot, whether someone might be behind one of the other doors. I was just getting edgy when I heard Ida coming down the hall, talking to someone. "I don't know yet," she was saying. "Let's take it one day at a time. Trust me on this. I'll come up with a plan."

"What?" asked another female voice. "To cut back further on materials? Snacks? What's your plan exactly?"

"Look," Ida said. Their footsteps had stopped just outside the door. "We'll find a way to drum up some new business. And if we can't, I'll take it from my own—"

"You're crazy," the other interrupted, but then Ida threw the door open. "This is Flo Newberry," she said quickly.

Flo Newberry was a tall, thin woman, older than Ida, with short gray hair pushed back behind her ears. She closed her mouth when she saw me and made an attempt to smile. When she extended her hand, I stood up to shake it. "Flo's my partner," Ida said. "Flo, this is Ginny Jarrell. She's one of the girls who was with the Sturbridge girl when—"

"Oh," Flo interrupted. She put her fingertips to her thin lips and her features clustered with concern. It occurred to me that she looked something like Herman Gardener's unfortunate wife.

"I'm so sorry," Flo said.

Ida, who was apparently resigned to getting the formalities over with, sighed. "Ginny's isn't talking," she said.

"Really?" asked Flo, and she took a step back.

"No, I don't just mean now. I mean she hasn't talked for some weeks. It's her response to the . . . uh . . . accident."

Flo nodded, tried in vain to smile, then turned to Ida. "I don't see how—"

"I'm not sure either. But I'd like to give it a shot. What do you say? Will you do this for me?"

Flo turned her head aside to consider. Ida and I stared where she was staring, at the shelves that lined the far wall. They were full of canned goods, everything from tomato paste to Dinty Moore stews. On the floor more cans had been packed into paper bags, and on each bag a surname had been printed in black magic marker. "Okay," Flo conceded at last. She stuck her thin hand out at me and I shook it once again. "Welcome aboard," she said without any trace of enthusiasm.

8

Ida Newet never explained to the children, and none of them ever asked—at least not when I was around. She took me aside each afternoon when I came in after school and showed me the projects that I would be helping them with. Then she left it to me to figure out how to convey the information.

The children sat at three long tables, two for the three- and four-year-olds who were there all day, and one for the older kids who came in when I did. The older ones quieted down right away when I stood at the head of their table with my arms stuffed full of sandwich bags and lengths of colored yarn and scissors and glue. In fact, some regarded me suspiciously, I thought, as if my silence enabled me to hear their most secret thoughts. I would pass around the sample that Ida had provided me with, a paper-bag raccoon stuffed with newspaper or a white dove with its wings glued on at angles, and when it came back to me, I would demonstrate the first few steps myself. Then I would pass out the materials and let them try on their own. Miss Ginny, they called me when they got into trouble. Then I would go to stand behind the bungler, and while his eyes shifted uneasily between my hands and the faces of the others, I would point out the mistake and show him how to rectify it.

The younger children were more difficult to work with. Having been there all day, they were hardly aware of their surroundings by the time I arrived, let alone of me. Some kept their heads on the table while I demonstrated, others whined and fretted, and one or two stuck their fingers in their noses, trying to enliven their companions by holding the results of their dig in their faces. Nor were their projects as sophisticated as those of the older kids. For the most part they were one-dimensional, fish or flowers to color and then to cut out. The kids who could stay in the lines tended to choose black or brown crayons. The ones who were inclined toward more festive colors were often satisfied simply to scratch lightning bolts across their papers. As none of them could be persuaded to take their time with the cutting—though I could hardly blame them when their scissors were so blunt—fins, leaves, and all other projections were discarded along with the scrap.

Yet Ida was unfailingly enthusiastic about everything they did. "Oh, how lovely," she would cry, and then she would point out what was unique in each of them. "You've learned to mix colors!" she exclaimed once when a little boy who had begun with a green fish had a change of heart and scribbled yellow over it. "Does everybody see this? Green and yellow make blue. Thomas discovered that, all by himself."

The children brought the completed projects to a table at the far end of the dingy basement, where the supplies were kept. Between it and the wall behind it there were several huge flattened cardboard boxes, the kind in which appliances come packed. Ida planned to cut them along the folds, and then have the older children paint mountains on the pieces. I had written her a note one day, to ask why she didn't just buy poster board, which would be easier to paint on and uniform in size. But the key word, of course, was "buy," and I never bothered to show it to her. Likewise, the paint cans, which were lined up beneath the table, had come from Ida's and Flo's basements, the pastel remnants from children's rooms, trim paints, and several different shades of white.

I was sitting back there one afternoon, collecting sequined butterflies from the three-and four-year-olds and turning each over to make sure there was a name on it, when the pastor of the church came down, almost scaring me to death with his bulk, his loose black frock, and his noiselessness. He paused at the bottom of the stairs for a moment, with a finger on his lip, smiling behind it, waiting, I suppose, for an invitation. Then, in spite of the fact that Flo, whose jaw had fallen, did not invite him in, he moved forward, slowly, looking over the children's shoulders as if someone had appointed him to oversee their work.

Ida had been bent over one of the boys, but when she saw him approaching between the tables, she straightened and greeted him. He returned her cheerful greeting with a nod. When he had passed her, she followed him. "Forgive me my inquisitiveness," he said without turning. "I hear the children, but I never see them. I couldn't restrain myself any longer."

When he had gone the length of the work tables, his gaze fell on the table in the back where I was standing. From where he stood, the piles of projects must have looked like mounds of litter. He cocked his head, squinted at them, and then came forward for a better look.

When the parents came to pick up their children, Flo brought them a clipboard and had them sign out. This formality—unnecessary since we knew all of their faces—intimidated them, and they lingered near the doorway while Flo collected their offspring. The pastor was the first man that I knew of to actually cross the basement floor. What right had he? He had no child here. The day-care center, Flo had told me, had nothing to do with the church, no affiliation at all. We simply rented space from them. I tried to make eye contact with Ida, to relate my indignation, but she was prancing at his side now, wringing her hands and smiling moronically while she waited for his response to the projects.

Finally, he began to rave, which further infuriated me. He simply couldn't believe that such wonderful things were happening right in the basement of his very own church. He said it was like finding out that Santa's elves had quit the North Pole and come to work in Rock Ridge without his knowing it—an inappropriate simile, I thought, for a man of the cloth. He picked up a paper-bag bunny. One of its ears had fallen over and its cotton-ball tail was dangling by a single fiber. "I'd love to give this rascal a home upstairs in my office," he said.

Ida bit her lip. "Oh, Father, I'm sure the children would love to have you adopt some of their animals, but you'll have to wait until Christmas."

He put the bunny back and turned to look at her. "What happens then?"

Her eyes flashed with pride. "Well, we're going to make a

display, a kind of replica of nature right here in your basement. It'll be ready for our Christmas party, which will be the last school day before the vacation." She took a step closer to him. "The parents enjoy it as much as the kids do," she confided.

The pastor turned from her to survey the table again, probably wondering, as I had many times, how Ida would manage to assemble all this junk in such a way as to replicate nature, unless it would be at its very worst—a hurricane, earthquake, or some other natural disaster. "All God's gifts," Ida added encouragingly, "for all the parents to come and see."

He turned back towards her and nodded, as if he was beginning to understand. "Yes," he mumbled, "because we're made so that we love first when we see them painted . . ."

Ida screwed up her face, confused. Although his back was to me, I imagined that he was smiling at her, condescendingly. As he didn't bother to inform her that he had been quoting, I extracted a purple crayon from Peter, the little boy who was standing beside me, and scribbled *Browning* on the back of his butterfly and held it up for Ida to see. But Peter noticed first and exclaimed, "Hey, that's not my name!" so shrilly that the pastor turned abruptly to see what the commotion was about.

He looked at me, directly, for the first time. "I have an idea," he said suddenly, turning back to Ida. "How about setting up your replica of nature up in the church, where not only the parents but my whole congregation can admire it? Would you consider doing that?"

When Ida didn't answer right away, he added, "Think of how good it would be for business. You've got plenty of room down here, and I've got plenty of parishioners who send their children as far away as Centertown for day care. If they saw the kind of work you were doing . . ."

"I'll have to talk to Flo," Ida said gingerly, "but it might not be a bad idea."

Since I had nothing else to spend my money on, it took me only three weeks to accumulate the $160 that I had decided would be sufficient. I prepared two notes, the first of which said only, *I need to talk to you alone.* I handed it to Tom Heely not in the cafeteria, where he would surely have passed it around for the amusement of his friends, but in English class, where he had none. He opened it up immediately, read it, and nodded expressionlessly. When I looked away from him, I caught Terri dropping her gaze from our transaction.

He and Frankie were standing near my locker at the end of the day. As soon as they saw me approaching, they rolled their eyes and exchanged identical smirks. "I guess she changed her mind about going out with me," Tom Heely said for my benefit.

I put my books down to dig for my pen in my bag, but when I straightened up, Tom was holding a pen out for me, and a pad too on which he had written, *Yes or no, and if yes, your place or mine?* Frankie, who had leaned over to read it, laughed wildly.

"Look," I said, my voice hoarse from disuse, "you've got a brain. You know what 'alone' means. Get rid of him."

Tom looked startled for a second, but he recovered quickly, resuming his smirk. "You heard her," he said to Frankie, who was still laughing. "She wants to be alone with me."

Frankie turned and went down the hall, shaking his head, and I handed the second note to Tom.

It was written in pencil—printed, actually—and unsigned; no one could prove that I had written it. He took it over by the window, into the shaft of sunlight there. When I saw his smirk vanish, I knew he had finished and I snatched it back. "Why?" he said.

I only stared at him; it was none of his business.

"No way," he said. "I'm not into that."

I wrote on the back of the note, *I've got $160.*

"It's not the money," he said.

Okay, forget it, I wrote.

I picked up my books and turned to my locker. He waited, quiet for once, while I finished up my business. "Listen," he said. "All kidding aside, I'd really like to get to know you better. I think we've got stuff in common."

"What?" I whispered. I was too defeated to muster the energy to write.

"We both like Wordsworth," he said, and he offered me a half smile that would have been touching on any other face. "I don't go out with drug dealers," I replied, and I started down the hall. "You've got balls, girl, after what you just asked me for!" I heard him cry out behind me.

I had no alternative plan unless I could convince Tom Heely in the days to come, which I fully intended to try to do. Otherwise, I had saved up the money for nothing. I stood at the top of the stairs entertaining the idea of giving up my job in the basement below, although for only a moment. The truth was that I liked it. I liked the kids and I liked Ida, and even, most of the time, Flo. And besides, I had nothing else to do in the afternoons. If not for everything that had happened, Sharon, Terri, and I might have joined some of the after-school activities by now, the debate team or the chess club (yes, they had eventually got me to play), or maybe even gone out for girls' soccer. But Sharon was gone, Terri might as well have been, and I myself had no more desire to be in the building when the greater din was gone than I had to be exposed to the whims of passers-by out on the sports field. In the church wing I felt safe, or nearly so.

As if he had read my thoughts, the pastor appeared in the hall just then, having come out of his office, his brows furrowed in concentration and his head bent. I turned to hurry down the stairs, but he noticed me and called out, "Miss, wait!"

I poked my head back out. Now he was smiling and holding out some papers. "What a coincidence. I was just praying that God would send someone to help me out. . . ."

I shook my head to let him know that either he or God had made a huge mistake, but his smile didn't falter. "You work downstairs, right?"

I nodded.

"Listen, we've got this food in there." He thumbed in the direction of the conference room. "All these canned goods that parishioners have donated. They have to be delivered before Thanksgiving to the poor people in the area. I rounded up two boys to help me, but one gets lost every time he goes out and the other has never shown up at all. I'll pay you, of course."

In spite of the fact that I was flattered to think that he realized I was old enough to drive, I pointed at him, so as to ask why he didn't just make the deliveries himself. He looked so astonished that I expected him to say, "Who? Me?" but instead he whispered, "Don't you talk, dear?"

Something in his tone made me quake, and I had to gulp back what felt like a rising sob. Then I remembered Herman Gardener saying, "Are you all right, young lady?"

I shook it off. There was no resemblance between the two men. The pastor was twice his size, nosy, and condescending too. I took out my trusty pad and scribbled, *I've taken a vow of silence, temporarily.*

He beamed when he read it. "Why, then, you're just the one! The people who receive these donations don't necessarily want the public to know about it."

Yes, I thought, I'm perfect for the job. I imagined driving down a long dirt driveway, approaching a shack where one window was opened, the barrel of an extended gun swiveling to follow my path.

"You could use my car," he said.

I shook my head.

"It's a Toyota. Midnight blue, I think it's called. It has a tape machine."

When I shook my head again he looked up at the ceiling, as if in response to the voice of some unseen entity. "It's heated," he added.

I rolled my eyes. He laughed. "What's your name?" he asked.

I wrote it down.

"Ginny, listen, I need help. An hour a day, for the next three, after you get done downstairs, of course. You don't have to go into anyone's house, just leave the bags on their doorsteps. I promise you, you'll be rewarded for this, and I'm not just talking about the few dollars I'll be able to give you."

The notion of an intangible reward gave me pause, not that I actually believed in that stuff. But the fact was, Ida needed to attract more clients, so that she wouldn't have to continue paying me from her own paycheck, and now the pastor had come down and offered, when you got right down to it, free advertising. Had he been aware of her dilemma? Was he psychic? Nah, impossible, I decided. And I was about to put my pen to paper one last time when Ida came charging up the stairs.

"Ginny!" she exclaimed when she saw me. "Father, hello. Ginny, I was just about to phone your house. You're late!" She laughed and clapped her hand to her chest. "Not that I mind. That's not what I mean. I was worried."

"It's my fault," the pastor said, and he proceeded to explain his appeal.

Ida shook her head all the while. "Oh, father, I don't think that's such a good idea. I mean, not the part about giving food to the poor, obviously. I mean for Ginny to do it, to go to the houses of strangers. I mean, she's had some . . . well . . . disconcerting . . ."

She paused, biting her bottom lip. The pastor, meanwhile, looked at me with renewed interest.

"Oh, Ginny," she continued, her eyes darting back and forth between us. "I *am* sorry. Listen to me. I'm not your mother. Of course she can go if she wants to. In fact, I'll escort her. I drive her home anyway, so there's no big deal. We'll just make a few stops on our way. It'll be fun."

It was fun, actually, and more rewarding than the pastor could possibly have imagined.

Each evening, just before we closed up, the pastor came down for Ida's keys. Then he carried the bags out himself and placed them in the back of her vechile. He gave us a map on which he had marked each of our destinations with a red pen. The houses of the poor were not all in one area, as is the case in more suburban locales, but spread throughout Rock Ridge, many on back roads that I had never been to before. For our convenience, he tried to keep each night's deliveries in the same area.

Before we set out, we stopped at McDonald's for fries and sodas—something to tide us over until dinner, Ida said. The first night, I grabbed her arm when I saw that she intended to get out and go in. She understood immediately, closed the car door, and drove around to the drive-through window instead. After receiving our sack of food, we pulled over to the far corner of the lot and ate while she studied the map, determining the best way to proceed.

We chatted while we drove, or rather she did. As I wasn't expected to comment, I had the luxury of either paying attention or not. Ida was all atwitter at that time of day. "Did you hear how Philip squealed when I commented on how well he's staying in the lines lately?" she said, and, "Oh, that Pearl! What a sweetheart she is, bringing me in a sea shell to listen to after she heard me tell Flo how much I love the ocean."

When she was quiet, she smiled, so that I knew she must still be thinking about the kids. And when she changed the subject, it was usually to talk about her daughters, Lilly and Diane. She couldn't wait until Thanksgiving to see them. And I would see them too, she reminded me in a voice that suggested it would a blessing beyond measure, since Mom and I would be dining with the Newet family that day.

The first two evenings, Ida got out of the car, and because she didn't like the idea of leaving the goods on the stoop, where they might freeze or fall into the wrong hands, she rang the bell once before she departed. At one of the houses—a small cottage really—an old man with a rake appeared from behind a tree just as we were pulling into the driveway. He looked angry at first, but when he saw Ida getting out with a bag, his face lit up. He dropped his rake, rushed to take the bag, and then spent a full five minutes thanking her profusely. When she got back in the car, her eyes were moist. "You know what?" she said. "I'm going to make an extra pumpkin pie Thanksgiving morning and have one of the girls drive it over to him."

The goodwill thing was contagious, and I began to catch some of it myself. Sure, Bev's parents and brothers would be eating without her, and Herman Gardener alone with his daughter, and the waitress's husband with his two young children. Sure, it was probably all my fault (I didn't *really* believe in my anger theory, though I couldn't lose it either), but here I was, making up for it in some small way, paying my dues.

A few of the houses that we stopped at were small capes like my own, with well-raked yards and evidence that there had been summer gardens. More often we pulled up in front of shacks, cottages that had once been vacation cabins but had since been sold and were now in various stages of disrepair. Though we saw no shotguns, there were often barking dogs, and not all of the faces that appeared at the windows were friendly.

Our third night out was bitterly cold, and Ida, who was wearing her gray poncho with the two buttons missing at her throat, was working on a virus. She had had her inhaler in and out of her nose so many times during the course of the afternoon that her nostrils had actually widened, or so it seemed to me. So, when we arrived in front of a house that was completely dark, I stopped her before she could get out and pointed to myself. "Are you sure?" she asked.

I was quick about my business. Ida popped the hatch and I ran around the back and got out the bag for a Mrs. Davies. I deposited it on the stoop, rang the bell, and jumped back into the Four-Runner. Ida was just about to hit the gas when a light went on, and we saw the face of a little girl appear in the window. She looked at the bag on the stoop and then, bouncing up and down, probably on a sofa, waved deliriously. "You know," Ida said sadly, "I bet her mother isn't home. I bet she's been sitting in the dark waiting for her since she got off the school bus. She can't be more than what? Five? Six?" She shrugged. "Well, what do you do when you can't afford a sitter or day care?"

I knew what it was like to sit in the house with the lights off lest anyone should guess you are in. Mom and I had, at my insistence, done just that on Halloween. She was good about it at first. She put away all the candy she had bought, except the Milky Ways, which we planned to snack on, and we sat side be side on the sofa listening to the cars slow down in front of our house and then pull into the driveway of the house next door. But when the traffic let up, Mom began to complain. She was bored, she said. Couldn't she just put on one little light so that she could at least read a magazine? "No," I was forced to say since she wouldn't have seen my head shaking in the dark. She sighed. She had herself another Milky Way. Then she got up and made her way to her bedroom, her fingertips raking the walls, cursing when she bumped into things. When she returned, she was wearing the headband flashlight that Dad used to wear when he had to go under the sink to fix the pipes. "Will this do?" she asked. I couldn't see her face—she had the light tilted toward the ceiling—but I could hear in her voice that she was crying.

So empathetic was I to the child's plight that I thought I would volunteer to do the next house too—right up until we arrived in front of it. A shack in considerably worse shape than any that we had come across, it dipped severely on one side, so that I thought the foundation must be crumbling. Not that you could actually see the foundation, with all the tires, rusted appliances, and automobile parts heaped around it.

There were clotheslines strung between the house and the small dilapidated shed beside it, all laden with shabby garments, holey underwear, and stained stretched-out T-shirts that looked brittle enough in the freezing air to shatter. Scattered about the yard were plastic container lids, broken toys, beer cans, and plastic game parts. "Oh," Ida said as we turned to look at each other.

She got out, but she hesitated a moment, and I could see that she was scared too. Don't ring the bell, I wanted to call after her; just put down the bag and run.

At first, when she turned from the stoop, I thought she would, but then I saw that she was only coming back to the car for a second bag. This was our first two-bag family, which meant, I assumed, either that they were especially poor or that they were exceptional in number. The shack could not have been more than fifteen feet in length. Where did they sleep?, I wondered, in sleeping bags all in a row?

Ida knocked, since there was no bell, and was just turning when I saw the curtain move, then a hand, and a face—a rough-looking man who was, apparently, shirtless. As if he had just tasted something bitter, his lips pulled back. He turned aside to say something to someone, I guessed, because just as Ida was getting back into the car, another face appeared, a boy my age. He looked out, his expression as disinterested as when Tom Heely had first pointed me out to him.

It was almost dark. We had our headlights on. I was slouched down in my seat. He couldn't have seen me.

The shack looked considerably worse in the daylight. The chimney, which was puffing smoke, was missing bricks, and some of the roof tiles lay on the ground. The window—there was only one that I could see—was so scummed up that it was a wonder that I had been able to recognize Frankie Stewart's face through it. What I had taken to be a curtain now appeared to be a length of fabric, a blue sheet which was probably tacked to the frame. The siding was uneven, and the red-trim paint was peeling badly. The small yard, which was enclosed by a chicken-wire fence, was shrubless and treeless. But the worst thing about the house was a kind of blatancy about its disorder—maybe because no effort had been made to cover the rusted appliances that surrounded it. Or maybe it only seemed so because it was so close to the road—as if its inhabitants were defying the passerby to make a judgment. I was scared, of course, but coming here meant I would have something on him; there was no other way to proceed.

I knocked and prayed that he would come to the door. If he didn't, I planned to smile as pleasantly as I knew how and to tell whoever did that I was from the church and had come to make sure that their food had been delivered. I didn't think they would try to harm anyone associated with the church. But just in case, I had in my shoulder bag a can of Mom's hairspray, with the cap off, and my fingertip fluttering on the nozzle.

The door opened a crack, and I saw one of Frankie's blue-gray eyes. "What the . . . ?" He bit down on the "f" and didn't say it.

"I need to talk to you," I said quickly. There was no time for passing notes. I had borrowed Ida's car and had promised to have it back to her within a half hour. "Do you mind stepping outside for a moment?"

He mumbled something, but with the door covering half of his face, I didn't get it. "Please," I said.

"I'm not dressed," he answered in a low, angry voice.

Involuntarily I moved my head, and before he could step

aside, I saw that he was wearing only cut-off jeans, very short and opened at the top. "Could you get dressed?"

"Wait a minute."

The door closed, then opened again. Now he was wearing the stained denim jacket that he wore to school every day. He was still shirtless and his feet were bare. "If this is about Tommy . . ." he warned.

I laughed at the thought, but I stopped when I saw that his face was utterly grave, his full lips not sneering as usual but motionless. He had his head turned slightly to the side; he wasn't even looking at me. "Are we alone?" I asked.

"Yeah." He flicked his head to get the hair out of his eyes. "So get on with it."

I took the twenties out of my jacket pocket and fanned them before his face. If they sparked any interest, he didn't show it. "I need a gun," I whispered. "A small one. Something I can fit in my bag. A pretty ivory handle, if you can get it."

He said nothing.

"You must have known," I continued. "I'm sure Tom told you."

"He told me you wanted to get something started with him and that he said no way."

"Oh, well, I guess he lied," I responded. He shrugged, and I shrugged back at him. "So, can you get it for me?"

"You want to kill someone?"

"Maybe." I smiled; I was trying to keep things light.

He released his hold on the door just long enough to touch his fingers to his head. "Oh, I get it. You want to kill someone and then let me take the rap for it? That's cute. That's real cute. Wait till the guys hear—"

His threat infuriated me and I took a step closer. "Wait till the guys hear what, Frankie? You get a delivery last night? Some food from the church? You want me to get you another bag? I can do that. I can bring it into school, right into the cafeteria. Or better yet, I can get some of my friends to drive me over here and—"

"Shut up, bitch," he said evenly. "I get the point."

I stepped back, stung. Nobody had ever talked that way to me before. Then I realized what I had said to him. I was shocked, horrified to find myself engaged in such a base performance, but equally incapable of doing anything about it. The one thing I didn't want to do was cry, but I felt the tears welling up nevertheless. I turned and looked at Ida's car, then pivoted back to face him.

"I never would have said where I got it from," I cried defensively. "I'm not like that. You don't even know me. And I'm not planning on killing anyone. I just want it for protection, for my mother and me. We live all alone, and I was almost killed. You know that. Can you understand what that feels like? No, how could you? No one does. I was right there, and if . . ."

I realized I was rambling and stopped to catch my breath, but it was too late; I had lost all control. "I hate you," I cried. "You're just the kind of mean person who winds up . . ."

I stopped myself in time to hear him mumble, "No, I'm not."

We stood in silence for a few moments, not looking at each other. I stared at his hand on the door, at his knuckles, white with cold or anger. "I got an older brother," he said at last. And then, as if that explained everything, he unclenched his fingers and his palm turned upward. I put the bills into his hand. His fingers closed around them. "I'll take this as a deposit for him," he said.

"A deposit? That's $160. How much more do you think you'll need?"

"Three hundred."

"I can't get that much. Or I can, but it will take forever. I want to do this now. And how do I know you won't just keep it, and then laugh in my face like that day with Tom Heely?"

I saw his lips writhe in contempt. "What was that bit about bringing your friends here?" he whispered. "I'd call that blackmail. What do they call it over on your side of Rock Ridge?"

I looked down at my feet, deeply ashamed. "Blackmail, I guess, would be accurate."

"Well, at least we understand each other. Now go. Get the hell out of here."

9

We got off to a rough start Thanksgiving morning. There were some eighty wooded acres behind our house, all owned by an elderly woman who never permitted any hunting on her property. When I awoke and went to the window, however, I saw a flicker of red, a hunter's hat, deep in the woods. I wrote a note suggesting that Mrs. Peterson be called immediately and awakened Mom, who liked to sleep late when she didn't have to go to work. She told me to mind my own business and then, after she'd had her coffee, and as if she thought I had only been imagining, she started in again about me seeing a therapist.

I hardly heard a word she said; I was too busy looking out the window, checking for footprints in the light snow that had fallen.

Then later, when we were baking our respective contributions for Ida's dinner, my grandmother called. I could tell right away that it was her because Mom stopped what she was doing, pulled a chair into the corner, and spoke with her back turned half toward me. She kept an ashtray on her lap and puffed on a plastic cigarette the entire time. With her legs curled under her and her long hair hanging in her face, she looked like the little girl Grandma's phone calls always reduced her to. Grandma fired questions and Mom answered in a thin, whiny voice that I was not usually accustomed to hearing. "Thirty thousand . . ." Mom said, "three hundred . . . two forty-nine round trip."

Grandma was of the opinion that my father should have been turning his advances over to Mom, that *she* should have been giving *him* an allowance from them and not the other way around. She must have been sitting there in her Sunrise condo with a calculator on her lap, lamenting the fact that we had not been able to afford to fly down for Thanksgiving, and then calculating how much more Mom would need to extract from him to insure that we got down for Christmas. She was a bitter woman, twice Mom's size and as strong as a horse. An Italian whose husband (now deceased) had been a mason, she trusted no one who worked with his head instead of his hands. She had been telling Mom from the getgo that she had no business marrying a writer, that either he wouldn't make it (he was a copywriter for an ad agency back then) and would thus be frustrated and hard to live with, or he *would,* and then he'd drop her for the first woman who caught his eye.

Before it happened, Mom despised her of course, and then even for some months afterwards. Once enough time had elapsed though, they fell back into what must have been their relationship when Mom was a little girl—which is to say that Mom complained and Grandma spewed her poisonous words at the objects of Mom's vexations. "We'd be eating all alone if not for Ida," I heard her say. "Yes, that's right, all alone . . . no, you're right, he doesn't care . . . why should he?"

This was a side of Mom that I didn't like to see. I guess she didn't either, because after they hung up, Mom was always downcast and self-effacing.

Now she tasted the sweet-potato casserole that she had been working on so happily all morning and made a face. "This isn't going to work," she said tartly. "Why don't you just give it to Surge and save me the embarrassment of having to see it on the table with all of the wonderful stuff that Ida makes." She pushed her hair behind her ears and tightened the belt on her bathrobe. "In fact, I've got a better idea. Why don't you just go on without me. They'll be so merry over there with the twins home and everything . . . I'll just bring them down."

She slumped out of the kitchen, and I was left alone to consider my own concerns. I hadn't slept well. I was still having terrible dreams, sometimes about the day at the diner and sometimes based on the newspaper articles that I read. I shouldn't have been reading them, I knew, but like the arachnaphobic who cannot keep from going to the back of the pet shop to look at the tarantulas, I couldn't help myself. Lately, I had begun to have another sort of dream as well, and in some ways these puzzled me more than the frightening ones. I had begun to dream about boys. They stalked my subconscious, opening doors, calling out my name. Some of them held their hands behind their backs, so that I suspected that they might be concealing boxes of candy or bouquets of flowers. Some were boys from school, the popular, ultra goodlooking ones who never talked to me. Others were strangers. None seemed particularly threatening, but then why was I always hiding? I was so alone without Terri and Sharon that you'd think I would have been happy to have suitors, if only in my psyche, but I wasn't. The dreams troubled me.

When Mom slumped back into the kitchen, some twenty minutes later, she had dressed in her favorite gray sweat suit, and had put on her dolphin earrings and combed her hair. "Aren't you ready yet?" she snapped. She went to the refrigerator, removed her casserole which I had put away for her, and then stood with her arms folded, and her eyes, which were puffy and red, fixed on me until I was done with my baking and ready to go.

"So," Mom said, "what's new?" and she laughed nervously. Charles pursed his lips like duck bills. "Oh, not much really. You know how it is. I work, I eat, I sleep."

"He's doing yoga," Ida called cheerfully from the kitchen.

Mom already knew that of course, and Ida knew she knew, because she had told her some time ago, but Mom pretended to be pleasantly surprised anyway. "Yoga, really?" She picked up her wine glass and took a sip.

We were sitting in the family room, which had been decorated to look like it hadn't been. Most of the furniture was blonde, but a few darker pieces had been thrown in to create an illusion of indifference. Likewise, the lamps on the end tables were not a set, but if you looked carefully, you realized that the same colors ran through them, green and a kind of pinkish gold. It was all new, all from Ethan Allen, Ida had told Mom, who hadn't been to the house in over a year.

The twins were not about. Lilly was upstairs, talking to

some friends on the phone, and Diane was out delivering the pumpkin pie that Ida had baked for the overly appreciative old man who we had encountered the other night. Charles glanced nervously at the door. As he was usually talkative, I couldn't tell whether it was Mom being here without my father or something else that was making him edgy. "I'm not the only one taking it," Charles said.

"It's everyone, all his employees," Ida called from the other side of the snack bar where she was taking things out of the refrigerator and setting them down along the counter.

Mom turned back towards Charles. She had asked to help several times, but Ida wouldn't hear of it. "So," she said, "your whole company is taking yoga classes?"

"Yes, we got this woman in . . ." He glanced at me. " . . . And she's been giving instructions over lunch hour."

"You mean, so instead of eating—"

"Oh no. Can you imagine what the reaction to that would have been? What I did was extend the lunch hour to an hour and a half. That way we can all do yoga for a half hour, and then we still have time to eat afterwards. Her theory, this woman's, the instructor's, is that the half hour lost from work time will be more than compensated for by our proficiency when we do get back to business. That's what sold me, actually."

"And, so, is it working?"

"Yes, in fact. It *seems* to be." He laughed. "In any case, everyone seems happier."

Mom laughed too, with some ease this time. "It might be that they're just happy to have an extra half hour tacked on to lunch."

"Is that any way for a devoted Tai Chi student to talk?" interrupted Ida as she carried a dish of cranberry sauce into the dining room.

"I guess Ida told you I've been taking Tai Chi," Mom continued. "That's almost the same. I like to think of it as yoga in motion."

Charles sat forward. "Well, actually, I knew about Tai Chi from that Bill Moyer show and from Ida telling me that you were taking it. So when she first called, this . . . ah . . . woman, I asked her about it and she said that Tai Chi doesn't really

incorporate the breathing techniques that you use in yoga.
The effects of Tai Chi are more subtle, while yoga produces
quicker results. So I decided to go with her, this woman."
  "Does this woman have a name?" Mom asked.
  Charles smiled, then glanced at me. "Of course she does,"
he replied, but he sat back in his chair and didn't say it.

With the exception of Mom's sweet-potato dish and a loaf
of home-baked bread which was so hard it could have been
considered a weapon (which I made, but those who knew
were too polite to mention it and those who didn't were too
polite to ask), the dinner was wonderful, foodwise, and awkward at every other level. We began with a Circle of Thanks,
Ida's idea, in which each of us was asked to express our ap-
preciation for at least one thing besides the dinner itself. Ida
went first, saying that she was thankful for Charles; Diane
was next and thankful for Boston; Lilly was thankful for
some thing or some one called Poke (nobody dared to ask);
Charles was thankful for his business (Ida looked stung, but
only briefly); Mom was thankful for the entire Newet family;
and I was thankful, much to her delight, for Mom. As it
didn't seem any more appropriate for me to bring my pad
to the table than it would have been for Mom to bring her
ashtray and plastic cigarette, I was limited to hand signals, so
she was the only thing I *could* be thankful for.
  Diane and Lilly asked me a few questions, but my head
movement responses clearly made them uncomfortable, so
before long they gave up on me and tried to stay tuned to
the older generation's conversation. When there was a lull,
the twins spoke about some of the things that went on in
Boston, toning them down, I could tell, for their parents'
sake.
  I hadn't really known the twins that well before they went
off to college. They were two years older than me, and by
the time our parents became close friends some seven or
eight years ago, they were old enough to stay home when Ida
and Charles came to our house. When I was dragged along
to the Newets', the twins never seemed to be about. "Why
don't you go look for them?" Mom would encourage me. But
when I went upstairs, the giggling coming from behind Lilly's

door, which was where the second TV was, intimidated me, and I would wander into Diane's room instead and jump quietly on the edge of her bed until I heard someone coming.

"I've decided to change my name," Lilly announced as she scooped up more vegetables.

"Oh, you have, have you?" Charles cried out. The adults had all had their share of wine by then and were getting louder by the moment.

"I'm serious, Daddy. What kind of a name is Lilly for me?"

Mom nearly spit her food out laughing. "What, are you so sinister?"

Lilly smiled, not quite politely, and turned her attention back to Charles. "I mean it Daddy, legally," she whined. "Lilly is a name for someone with light hair and light skin. Look at me."

We all did, except for Diane who had just rapped her knuckles on a slice of my bread and was puffing her cheeks with repressed laughter. Lilly was right, I thought. With her long black hair and olive skin, she looked more like a raven than a white flower. "I was thinking of something like Dolores or Donna," Lilly said.

"Oh, Donna, oh, oh, Donna," Charles sang in an exaggeratedly deep voice.

Ida joined him. "I had a girl, Donna was her name . . ."

The twins, who had phone calls to make to their old high school buddies, disappeared soon after the meal. They had taken their plates into the kitchen, but neither had offered to help with the cleanup and Ida, whose face was by now pink, didn't seem to mind. So it was just the three of us, Mom and Ida and me in the kitchen, trying to organize the dishes in the sink and figure out what to do with all the leftovers. Charles was in the family room, standing in front of the TV, gesturing and shouting out orders to the football players. "Things seem better," Mom whispered.

Ida turned abruptly from the sink and put a wet hand on her wrist. "Oh, they are," she whispered back. "I didn't get a chance to tell you yet, but we're going to charter a sailboat sometime around Christmas. Just the two of us. Somewhere in the South."

Mom placed a hand over hers and squeezed. "Oh, darling, I'm so happy for you. How romantic that'll be."

"And I get to be the captain," Ida added, glancing at Charles in the family room. "Remember when I took those sailing classes last year? It's the one thing I know more about than he does."

"See," Mom chirped, "I told you everything would be all right. You were imagining all this time, making yourself sick for nothing."

"Yes!" Charles shouted.

We all turned to look at him. He had his fist up in the air, and his face was so full of joy that he looked as if he might cry. On the screen, several men were piled up in the snow. Beyond them, the crowds in the bleachers were rising, cheering, applauding the clash. "Touchdown?" asked Mom.

"I suppose," Ida said. Then she pulled Mom closer. "We had this really big fight, see, about not doing things together anymore? You know we hardly ever go out, and I thought, That's it, I can't take it anymore, he can't stand the sight of me. And I was just about to call and ask you for the number of your therapist when he comes in from work, puts his arms around me, and tells me about this idea . . . this boat thing. Don't say anything about it yet. We only just began to discuss it. I mean, it might not even come to pass. The twins were invited to spend Christmas skiing with a friend in Vermont. If that falls through, of course we wouldn't go. But that's not the point. Whether we go or not almost doesn't matter. The point is that he thought of it, that he *likes* me enough to want to spend an entire week with me . . . alone . . . on a boat no less!"

What does Goliath do? I wrote. Then I realized my mistake and scratched out *Goliath* and wrote *Rita* above it.

I was at my father's apartment. I had left Mom watching football with the Newets and promised to return to pick her up in an hour. My father had been watching football too when I came in—alone, thankfully—but he turned the set off as soon as he saw me, and gave me a hug from which, for some minutes, there was no escape.

Now we were sitting in the kitchen, across the table from

each other. His computer was there of course, along with an empty aluminum TV dinner tray, so that I knew that he had spent most of Thanksgiving either working or playing one of his many computer games. He read my note and then tapped a finger on it. "Is this why I don't see you anymore, Ginny?"

You know I'm working, I wrote on another sheet.

He sighed, then smiled half-heartedly and scratched his ear. I could see that I was going to have to help him along. *Is she a yoga instructor?* I wrote.

"Charles?" he asked.

I nodded.

He sighed again. "Did he? . . ." he began.

No, I wrote. *He didn't mention it to Mom. He just said he had an instructor and I figured it out.*

As if to encourage an elaboration, he looked at my hand. I put my pencil down and folded my hands on the table.

"All right," he said. "All right. I said something to Charles one day over lunch, to the effect that it was difficult meeting . . . people . . . when you sit at home all day in front of a computer. This was before Rita ever called him."

He lit a cigarette and sat for a moment with his head turned aside, his cheek resting on his thumb. "Rita had been a dancer for several years, but she never really made enough money to support herself; she always had to have other jobs. So then she got the idea to teach yoga, which she had always practiced and has some sort of a degree in."

He stopped to take a drag of his cigarette, then stubbed it out. "She was giving classes in her living room at first, but the apartment wasn't big enough. She couldn't afford to rent space, so she started calling local businesses to see whether there might be a need for that kind of thing. Charles was one of those she called."

He clasped his hands together, rubbing them vigorously. "And then he called me. He said he had this very nice single woman coming in to teach yoga for a half hour a day and did I want to meet her. She's a friend, Ginny. You can't expect me to sit in this apartment day after day, night after night . . ."

What about Mom? I wrote.

"Your mother is still very angry with me."

She sent you the cookies.

"Yes, she did," he said, and he bent his head over the table as if the thought disheartened him. Then he got up, went to the refrigerator, and took out a container of milk. "How 'bout I make us some hot chocolate?"

I nodded. His offer, I assumed, implied that he would have more to say about Mom, that he just needed a moment or two to collect his thoughts.

He moved about slowly. His thick wavy hair, which was long enough to cover the back of his neck, was entirely gray and his posture was not great, probably from years of hunching over a computer. From the back, you might easily mistake him for an old man. But when he turned and you saw his face, you were pleasantly surprised. He was rugged-looking, with a taut, wide jaw. His hands were big, with long fingers, and his eyes were narrow and steady, a penetrating blue which I, unfortunately, had not inherited. He looked great on the jacket of his last book—a novel about a fisherman who just got in his boat one day and never turned back. (Mom and I should have known then what was coming.) The photo was in black-and-white and Dad, who was wearing a dress shirt and a tie with faded blue jeans, had his shirt sleeves rolled up, revealing his muscular forearms. The tie was loose, the shirt was opened at the collar, and his head was slightly cocked, so that the light accentuated the hard lines of his jaw and cheekbone. One reviewer, a woman, naturally, had said that the protagonist was no less robust and virile than the author himself.

After extracting the Nestlé Quick, he removed two spoons from the drawer. I found myself impressed, as I often was, with how soundlessly he did things. He was a quiet man— thoughtful, some might say. I didn't know, myself; he seldom shared his thoughts. Goliath, however, was loud, an in-your-face sort of woman. I couldn't imagine the attraction.

He got out the Cool Whip and floated a large spoonful in each of our cups. Then he sat back down at the table, smiling feebly. "This not talking thing," he said, tilting his head, "it worries me a little."

Mom used to say that he was the king of evasion, that no

one in Rock Ridge could change a subject as subtly as he did. *We were talking about Mom,* I wrote.

"No, we weren't talking, Ginny. That's the point. *I* was talking and *you* were passing notes. I don't know whether we can *have* a serious conversation that way, sweety. Your mother, as you know, would like you to see a therapist. And at first I didn't think it would be a good idea. But now . . ."

I held a finger up to stop him. I started to write something but then changed my mind and crumpled up the paper and threw it on the floor.

I heard the door open as I was flying down the catwalk, but he didn't call me back. I wanted to peel out of the parking lot, so that he would know just how angry I was, but it took me a moment to get the car door unlocked, and although I popped the clutch, the Yugo only rattled in response. I recalled that Mom was the one who had taken that picture of him for his last book. She'd made him sit on a stool in the middle of the living room. "God, you're good-looking," she'd said. He'd smiled. Then she'd snapped. And right up until he finally confessed, Mom had taken credit for the look of self-possession she'd achieved with the shot.

I put the pedal to the floor, but I couldn't get the needle to do more than throb near fifty. I screeched my way around a bend in the road and almost hit the owl that was swooping across it.

I drove into my own neighborhood, past Sharon's house. (I still had her statement excerpt—if that was what it really was—in my bag. I had shown it to no one. And Terri, through her avoidance of me, had made it clear that she didn't want to discuss it either.) There were no lights on; they'd probably all gone to her grandmother's. I drove past Terri's. The lights were on there, but there was a car in the driveway with Texas plates. Evidently her sister Jill, who I didn't much like, was up for the holiday.

I turned on Glen Road, then Hill. As I was nearing my own house I heard Surge barking. Like Mom, he'd been having bladder problems lately. We had left him outside, chained to a tree so that he wouldn't be tempted to go off into the woods and sample some of the viscera that the hunters always left behind. My first inclination was to pull into the driveway, just to make sure that he hadn't gotten himself all tangled up. As I came closer, however, I realized that his barking was not the half-hearted greeting that he extended to passersby. He was barking fiercely, investing everything he had in it. Someone had to have been in our yard, or worse, in our house. I recalled the hunter that I had seen in the morning. Images jammed together in my head. I hit the gas and raced for Ida's.

I was a wreck by the time I arrived. There had been no car in the driveway, no cars in the road. Whoever it was that was stalking us had come on foot, probably from the woods behind the house. There were prisons in our area from which sometimes convicts escaped and took shelter in the woods. Once someone held a family hostage until the road blocks were removed and he felt it safe to proceed to more populated areas in search of anonymity.

I threw open the door and was hit with a blast of music which I recognized, in spite of my state, as Meatloaf's *Bat out of Hell*. Mom and Ida were in the corner of the room, dancing to it with more abandon than I would have thought either of them capable of. Charles was standing in front of the TV, which was also blaring. The wrong team made a touchdown, apparently, for Charles angrily clapped a fist into his palm.

"Someone's broken into our house!" I screamed.

Ida smiled and waved for me to come and join them. Mom, who couldn't have heard me over all the noise, did a thing with her hips which I guess she thought was cool. I dashed to the stereo, thumbed some buttons until it went off. Ida's mouth dropped open while Mom glared at me. "Thank you," Charles said.

"Someone's at our house!" I cried.

Mom's lips quivered moronically. "You're talking," she whispered.

"I was coming back from Dad's and I went past our house and Surge was barking."

"He barks all the time," Ida said. She went to the TV set, lowered it.

Mom came towards me with her arms outstretched. "My baby. Let me hold you."

I ducked her and rushed to Charles, who was looking back and forth between me and the football game. "Please, call the police."

Charles made a face. "You can't call the police on Thanksgiving."

"Charles!" Ida cried.

"It's hunting season," he snapped. "It was probably just someone coming back from the woods."

"Did you actually see anyone?" Ida asked.

The twins came bounding down the stairs. "What's going on?" they asked in unison.

We piled into the Four-Runner, all six of us, with Charles at the wheel. He drove fast, not because he had begun to see this as an emergency but because he was in a hurry to get back to what must have been the third football game of the day. His lips were pressed together, and every now and then he gave his head a little shake of exasperation. The twins and Mom and I were all squeezed together in the back seat. Mom had her arm over my shoulder, but she was stiff, and I could tell it was not a gesture of love as much as one of necessity.

I was quaking as violently as I had under the table in the diner after the shots had been fired. I wanted to insist that we go to the police station, let them handle it, but I had lost my tongue—and perhaps my mind as well, for my thoughts were sketchy. I had the feeling that this was all preordained, that nothing I could say or do would change it.

Then I understood why. I had experienced many emotions since the day of the killings—grief, frustration, despair among them. But until tonight, until my father's attempt to circumvent my concerns by inventing some of his own, I hadn't really been angry. Even the night that I had met Goliath I had been more surprised than anything else. Now here I was, angry again, not only at my father but at all of them.

It was going to happen again. Again, I had unleashed the anger that my father instilled in me and let it loose on others. Think good thoughts, I told myself, let it go. But when Charles shook his head again, I realized that if I had been behind him instead of Ida, I would have kicked the back of his seat.

Why should I be angry with the twins? I asked myself. It wasn't their fault that they'd shared the same womb for nine months, that they remained a unit to the exclusion of everyone else.

Diane whispered something to Lilly, and Lilly laughed. They were beautiful girls, tall and dark like Charles, but with Ida's flawless complexion. Although I'd seen no evidence of it myself, they were supposed to be very smart. Diane was majoring in economics, Lilly in anthropology. Lilly sat forward suddenly. "Ma, I'm taking your ankle bracelet back to school with me this time whether you like it or not. You know you never wear it."

As Charles pulled into our driveway, his headlights revealed a silhouette rising from the stoop. I buried my face in Mom's coat and held my breath. I heard Charles yank up the emergency brake and then throw open the door. I felt the car bounce as he jumped out of it and shouted, "Who goes there?"

One of the twins laughed.

"It's just a kid," Ida said.

I disengaged myself from Mom and looked. A figure was coming toward us, and Surge, who had been unchained, was at his side. Frankie Stewart stuck his hand out. "Mr. Jarrell?" he asked.

Charles turned. "It must be some friend of yours, Ginny."

Both twins were laughing uncontrollably now, and Ida turned around in the front seat to offer me a sympathetic smile. I tried to smile back at her, but the muscles in my face had gone slack from all the tension. Frankie bent down and peered in. "Ginny?" he said. "Ginny Jarrell? Are you in there?"

I felt Mom's body relax against me, and it occurred to me that maybe she hadn't been upset with me after all, that maybe she had also been afraid. "Why don't we all go in," she said weakly. "I'll make some coffee and Charles and Ginny's friend can watch what's left of the football game."

Emotionally depleted, I went directly to my room and listened from there to Mom, Ida, and the twins in the kitchen. Fortunately, Diane and Lilly had plans for the evening, and as soon as the game was over, they rushed their parents right out.

"Can I speak to Ginny?" I heard Frankie say.

"Third door on the left," Mom said. That she was cranky again was apparent in her voice. "Please leave the door open," she added after Frankie had already started down the hall. "We always ask that of her male visitors."

As if I had any.

He entered and spent a full minute looking around my room, his gaze pausing on the computer, the television, the bookshelf, and finally, the photograph of Sharon, Terri, Surge, and me that hung over my bed. Mom had taken it the year before, outside in front of the house. Sharon was sitting on the stoop, slouched over with her feet turned in and her arms crossed so that she looked as if she was in pain. Terri had bent to pet Surge, and I was posing with my hands on my hips and one toe pointed, cheerleader fashion.

"You're whacked," Frankie said.

He looked over his shoulder. Then he closed the door halfway. "What'd you tell those people? That Charles guy said you thought I was robbing your house. What are you, paranoid or something?"

He walked to my desk and pulled out the chair there. I had painted it white some years ago, and Terri, who was the most artistic among us, had painted little red roses on it. Frankie looked at them, curled his upper lip, and replaced the chair. He looked around for another place to sit, but other than the chair and the bed, where I was sitting, there wasn't any.

"I came to talk to you about the . . ." He cocked his head toward the living room. " . . . well, you know what about. I talked to my brother, and he said he could do it. But like I thought, he was gonna want to be paid for his trouble." He squatted down in front of me, I guess in an effort to get me to look at him. "But you know what, Jarrell, I ain't gonna do it anymore. And you know why? Because you're whacked. If you had had a . . ." He nodded, then whispered. " . . . a gun . . . tonight, I'd be dead. Is that right or not?"

It occurred to me that my mother might be listening, so I picked up the remote and clicked on the TV. The two men who appeared on the screen were arguing. One had a gun in his hand, holding it at his side and gesturing angrily with his free hand. While Frankie, who seemed to have forgotten that he had just asked me a question, stared at the screen, I retrieved my pad from the night table and was just about to scribble a response when his hand shot out and grabbed my wrist. "Don't start that writing bullshit with me, okay? You save that for your smart-ass friends in school. You want to say something to me, then you *say* it. I don't put up with that kind of shit."

He snapped my wrist and released it. Then he began to pace. "I can't believe this," he mumbled to himself. "First she tries to blackmail me, and, idiot me, I let her, and then she calls the Thanksgiving squad, and I got to sit and make small talk with some goofy character who wants to know how long we been going out every time a commercial comes on . . . And those two twin clowns, peeking in from the kitchen, giggling and whispering to each other . . ."

The door moved, and Frankie stopped pacing to stare at it. When he saw that it was only Surge, he smiled. "Well, your dog likes me at least." He got down on his knees and started swiping at him.

"He's old," I said. "Don't do that."

"What are you talking about? He loves it."

Indeed, he seemed to, growling and lurching at Frankie's arms, his tail wagging constantly. When Frankie finally stopped, Surge nosed him to get him going again.

"How did you get here?" I asked, sweetly I hoped, for I was intent on showing him that I had another side besides my "whacked" one. He was right: I had acted impulsively. But I knew that if I'd had a gun, I would have had more control. I was determined to get that across.

He was petting Surge now, in hard sweeping movements that went from the top of his head to midway down his back. "A friend dropped me."

"How are you getting home?"

He shrugged. "I'll walk."

"Our car's at the Newets'. It's not very far. If you want, we could walk over and get it and then I could drive you home. We could talk about all this on the way."

"No way. No offense, but I don't want anyone to see me with you. That's why I came all the ways over here tonight. I didn't want to be seen talking to you in school."

"Thanks," I said.

He went to stand up, but Surge wouldn't let him. His thumb, I noticed, was scarred, and two of his fingernails were dirty. "This isn't about looks or like that, Jarrell, so don't go getting . . . the way you girls get. This isn't about who you are now, sitting on your bed with your little feet not even reaching the floor, looking like you just lost your best friend."

"I did," I interrupted. "Two of them."

As I spoke, it hit me that Thomas Rockwell, similarly friendless, must have felt exactly as I did now. His neighbors had confessed that they hadn't bothered to speak to him at the pool, that he had always appeared to *want* to be alone. But maybe he hadn't. Maybe he went down there precisely because he hoped someone might speak to him, touch him in a way that would break the spell that had been cast on him. We were no different, he and I, I saw, except that he had snapped and I was only verging on it. I had never felt so miserable in my entire life.

"This is about who you are in school," continued Frankie, who hadn't heard my comment, "walking around with your nose up in the air. I don't want no one thinking I'm kissing up to you."

"There's no one on the roads at this hour, asshole. Everyone's home with their families. It's Thanksgiving."

"*I'm* an asshole?"

I looked away, so that he wouldn't see my lips quivering. I had never called a boy an asshole before. I had never called anyone that. I hadn't meant to say it, hadn't even known it was coming until I heard it myself. Yet for some sick reason, I was delighted with myself. I wanted to keep saying it: asshole, asshole, asshole, asshole. . . . I felt that if I did, it would get me laughing, and that laughing would get me crying, and that what I needed more than anything else in the world right then was a really good cry. "*You're* the asshole," Frankie said.

"No, *you* are."

"No, Jarrell. I'm just some poor chump who got born into the wrong family."

It was time to change the subject. Clearly, this would get us nowhere. "So, you have my money?"

"What money?" Surge was licking him now, and Frankie was turning his face from side to side to keep from getting it on the mouth.

"My deposit, asshole." I simply couldn't help myself.

"No, I don't have your deposit," he replied sarcastically, "because I didn't know until you pulled up with your friends that I was going to have to change my mind about doing it."

"Won't your brother be disappointed? I mean, $460 must have sounded like easy money to him."

"He'll get over it. What's his name?"

"Surge. Where exactly *is* my deposit?"

"My brother's got it."

"What if he won't give it back? What if he already spent it, asshole?"

"Then I guess you'll get your gun. And I guess I'll have to spend the rest of my life feeling some responsibility for the people you kill."

"I didn't realize you were such a moralist, asshole."

He shrugged. "You ever go away on vacation, stuff like that?"

"Sometimes, why? You want me to let you know so that you can stop by and rob the house, asshole?"

"Chill, Jarrell. I just thought maybe you would want someone to watch your dog for you, so just chill out." He put Surge's big head between his hands and shook it. "This is one fine dog, aren't you Sarge?"

"Surge."

"Whatever. Hey, how many pounds of dog food does he put away a week?"

Surge rolled onto his back and extended his legs up in the air, and Frankie, who was squatting over him, began rubbing his stomach. I had never realized that he liked to be petted that hard. "I have no idea, asshole."

"Listen, Jarrell. *If* it is too late—and I hope to God it's not, because you *are* whacked—and *if* my brother didn't already go ahead and spend the money, then we got this other matter to consider, namely what my cut's going to be. Now I have a suggestion that won't cost you a red cent."

"And what might that be, asshole?"

"You let me borrow your dog now and then. We had a real good time together tonight, didn't we, Sarge?"

He lowered himself to the carpet and spread his legs out. Surge stepped between them and sat. Frankie began scratching his chest, and the harder he scratched, the faster Surge's left leg twitched—as if there was some direct connection between them. "How come you don't mind me calling you asshole, asshole?" I asked.

Frankie shrugged without looking at me. "I guess cause I'm used to it. That's what my old man calls me."

"Ginny!" my mother called from the other room. Her voice was shrill. "Ginny, are you cursing in there?"

10

I'd never felt like this before, so I had nothing with which to compare it. In my imaginary conversations with Sharon, who would have been the one to know, she explained away my feelings with her customary objectivity: I was a victim and could relate only to others of my kind; I was reacting to the fact that she, Sharon, had deserted me, and thus I had chosen just the kind of boy she would have found despicable; I was reacting to the fact that my father had deserted me, and thus had chosen just the kind of boy *he* would have found despicable; shock (his father calls him *what?*) had set off some suppressed maternal instinct; I was losing my mind, and seeing that the way back was too strenuous, I had chosen someone who was likely to hasten my descent.

My initial reaction to Mom's query that Thanksgiving night was indignation; she must have been in the hall to have heard me. I clicked my tongue and sighed disgustedly, but when I looked at Frankie, I saw that he was not only bobbing with contained laughter but also that his brows were raised as if to invite me to share his amusement. We laughed aloud together then, a shared chuckle in which our eyes were briefly but genially linked. Some trace of laughter remained on his face a moment later when he stood up and reminded me that I was not to speak to him in school, that one way or another, he would be in touch.

However, after a long weekend spent thinking about him, I was so eager to make myself available for this looming encounter that on Monday I wrote a note to Mr. Lovet, who presided over my study hall, and asked to be freed from that period until Christmas so that I could do some research in the library.

Of course I never went to the library. I had my lunch at Bev's table with the others and then moved off to another table to await the arrival of the late-lunchers. The table I chose was at the front of the cafeteria, at some distance from the one in the back where Frankie and his friends ate. Four subdued sophomore girls sat at one end of it, all but oblivious to my sudden appearance at the other. I kept a book opened before me, and a soda. Whenever I took a sip, I looked in his direction.

The first day he didn't notice me. He had his back to me, and I was able to do no more than scrutinize the back of his neck, most of which was concealed by the stained collar of his denim jacket. The second day, however, he sat facing me, and midway through his lunch, he *did* notice me. I smiled then; I couldn't help myself. He looked away, pressed his lips together—pensively, I thought—and looked back again. I smiled once more, but this time when he looked away, it was for good.

His indifference continued in the days that followed, allowing me ample opportunity to reevaluate my initial impression of him.

His hair, for instance, was roughly cut and always slightly greasy. It was parted on one side, and the side opposite the part was longer than the other. He had a cap, a peaked gray woolen thing that looked like it was from the twenties, which he often wore in school—in spite of the fact that they weren't permitted. When he had it on, his hair stuck out in tufts. Those greasy tufts, I realized now, were so black they were nearly blue when caught in the sun coming in through the cafeteria windows.

He seemed to have only two pairs of jeans, neither of which fit him properly. One pair was too baggy—not in the way that was stylish at the time, but more in the way that hand-me-downs are. The other pair was cheap, thin, shiny, imitation denim, and they were tight—too tight, I had once thought. Now, however, I saw that they they revealed his thigh muscles nicely, and I longed for the days when he would wear them—usually the last three days of the school week. Likewise, his T-shirts were stretched out at the bottom, and sometimes you could see clothespin indentations on them.

The bagginess at the bottom, though, only enhanced the way they fit his shoulders, which were broad and straight.

His skin was light, and slightly pinkish. His brows were long, nicely arched, and very dark. His lips were long, full, lazy-looking, and highlighted by the shadow of the beginnings of a mustache above them and a small but deep indenture below. He looked at things—his lunch, his companions, and, though rarely, me—sideways, with his head slightly tilted. He laughed a lot, at things his companions said, but he seldom spoke himself, so that I guessed that he was not quite comfortable with his lunch mates, and I delighted to discover that we had this in common. When he wasn't eating, he sat back, as far back as he could without falling off the bench—probably so as to remain on the periphery of the conversation. His kept his knees far apart, one elbow on each of them and his hands together in between—not folded but one over the other with both thumbs sticking up. His eyes revealed more lid than anything else, and that, coupled with his full lips, gave him a look of indolence which I had found disgusting in the past but now thought incredibly appealing.

Surge, I knew, was the key to our relationship. So, on Friday, instead of going to the cafeteria, I went to Frankie's locker and taped an envelope to it. Inside was a note saying that Mom and I would be away all day Saturday, that he could come and take Surge if he wished, and that he should stop by my locker after school and let me know.

He didn't stop by—or at least not in the five minutes I had to spare before I boarded the school bus that would take me to work. Nevertheless, I felt certain that I would see him on Saturday.

Oh, the power of love—or whatever it was. I even found myself smiling at the day-care center, and I had more patience with the children than I had ever had before. When the little ones handed in their projects, I gasped (I had gone back to not talking after Thanksgiving) and stood with my brows up and my mouth opened until they looked up and discerned my delight. Nor was it feigned. They were cutting out clouds that day, and each sharp edge seemed not an error but an ingenious effort to indicate that theirs, like mine, was an altered perspective.

That evening, at home, I insisted on both washing and drying the dishes, and afterward, when Mom started in on me again about the therapist, instead of holding up a piece of paper saying, *NO WAY* (I kept one handy on top of the toaster oven), I sent her little notes saying, *I'll think about it; You may be right; It's definitely worth some consideration,* etc.

Even my father's relationship with Goliath no longer enflamed me quite so much. I compared the way he had looked when he had spoken about her—casual, composed, remote— with the way I imagined I looked when I thought about Frankie—idle smile, empty eyes, a look of blissful stupidity, I suppose—and concluded that he could not truly be in love. Goliath was just a passing thing. As he had said, I couldn't expect him to sit in that little apartment alone all day and night. He was practically agoraphobic. Maybe Goliath would bring him out of his shell. Once out, surely he would see the sense in returning to us.

I wrote Mom a note in the morning saying that Frankie was coming for Surge for the day. Why? she wanted to know. I wrote another, explaining that as she was going to be out all day and as I was considering going out too, I thought Surge would be better off spending the day at Frankie's than being tied to a tree in such nasty weather. Actually, it was quite nice out, chilly but sunny, just the kind of weather Surge liked best.

Mom asked me where I got the idea that she was going out. In fact, she said, she planned to stay home all day and tackle the laundry that had been accumulating for the last three weeks. I hit my head with my palm—my mistake, Mom—and volunteered to stay home and help her. But, I wrote, since Frankie was already on his way, we might as well let him take the dog.

Frankie appeared shortly thereafter, and as Mom was in the shower, I got to talk to him alone. And talk I did. I didn't want to incur his wrath again. He had borrowed his brother's dilapidated Chevrolet—its muffler had announced his arrival—and he planned to take Surge up into the mountains for a hike and a picnic. "Oh, he'll *love* that!" I exclaimed, though I remembered the lassitude that Surge had displayed the last time he'd been picnicking with Mom and Ida and me. He pulled me aside, so that I could feel the heat on my elbow where he cupped it, and asked me where my mother was. When I said that she was showering, he informed me that his brother had already spent the deposit and so he would be getting me the gun—though he himself still thought it was a "shitty" idea. He suggested we talk about it, maybe when he brought Surge back in the evening.

"Perfect," I said.

And perfect it was. Ida came over that evening. She was upset again, about some nasty remark that Charles had made about her cooking, and she and Mom were so preoccupied discussing it over Zinfandel that they hardly seemed to notice when Frankie and Surge arrived. I led them both to my room and all but closed the door behind them. Then I sat down on the carpet, so that Frankie would feel no reluctance about making himself comfortable on the bed. Surge, meanwhile, went to his rug and immediately fell asleep.

Frankie, whose cheeks glowed, told me, although reluctantly, about his day in the mountains. They had hiked up to the falls and had their lunch. They had seen two deer, one of them a buck, and Surge had chased a rabbit. Then Frankie sat forward, his elbows on his knees, his hands dangling, and got down to more serious business. The day I had come to his house, I'd said that I wanted a gun small enough to fit in my shoulder bag. What he wanted to suggest was that I keep it in my closet, up on a shelf. I said that I would, that I would be extremely careful, that I had really learned my lesson Thanksgiving night. He nodded, his gaze traveling around my room. "You got Nintendo?" he asked. "Mortal Combat? Or just that there?" and he jutted his chin in the direction of my computer.

"Just that," I said, and in response he spread the fingers of one hand, as if to say, Well, that's it then.

That was my cue. I jumped to my feet and insisted he have a soda before he went. Then I ran off to the kitchen before he could protest and returned with two sodas, a tray of egg salad sandwiches which I'd prepared in advance, chips, and

some stale Twinkies I'd found in the back of the pantry. I
turned on the TV and clicked the remote several times until
I saw his brows merge with sudden interest. There was a
murder mystery on the screen, and Frankie, who had been
on the edge of the bed, leaned back, and without taking his
eyes from the TV, reached out for a sandwich.

The following Saturday I invited him to come for Surge
again. This time I teased him and said that I couldn't imagine
my Surge, who was twelve years old, chasing rabbits and hiking as far as the falls. He looked insulted at first, as if he
thought I'd meant to insinuate that he was less than honest.
Then he saw what I was up to and smiled coyly. "What? You
don't believe me, Jarrell?"

"I'd have to see for myself," I said.

He considered this for a moment, then shrugged. "Whatever, I don't care."

I nearly froze to death that day, sitting on the cold rocks
at the top of the mountain, but it was well worth it. Frankie,
who had made it clear to me over our sandwiches the week
before that he didn't like talking about himself, broke down
and proved otherwise—which is not to say he came right out
and told me his story. Actually, it was more a game of Twenty
Questions, and, as in the game, he answered mostly yes or
no, or, more accurately, he shrugged or nodded. Nor was
there any continuity to our discussion: I accumulated my
information here and there over the course of the entire day
while he threw sticks for Surge, fetched sticks Surge couldn't
find, rubbed sticks together (as we had no matches) unsuc-
cessfully when he thought that Surge might be getting cold,
skimmed stones over the stream that meandered through
our mountain playground, kicked at leaves, displaced rocks
in his search for salamanders, and pursued a hundred other
futile endeavors.

I learned the following: Until he was five, he and his
mother and brother had lived out west, in some small town
in northern California. His parents had divorced when he
was a baby and he had had no recollection of his father at
all. His mother had it tough, raising two sons on a waitress's
salary, and because she worked nights, he and his brother

often had to fend for themselves. But in spite of all that, they were a happy family—right up until his father returned.

His father then made apologies for whatever it was that had gone down before (his mother had never explained) and asked his mother to give up her life of hardship there in California and come with him to New York. He said he was living in a little cottage with a great view, had a decent job, and that she could stay home and take care of the boys; she wouldn't have to worry about anything. A picture book ending, but really only the beginning.

"You saw the house," Frankie said, looking out over the valley into which he was pitching rocks—he wasn't much for eye contact. And his father's job turned out to be at the town dump, though it had a fringe benefit, because when no one was around, he got to root through people's garbage and find things to bring home.

His mother, of course, saw that she would have to return to work, and she landed a job cleaning office buildings. She smoked a lot, and they were both hard drinkers. She was under a lot of stress because they fought so much, and one day when Frankie was ten she had a heart attack and died.

Then his father had an accident: a backhoe slipped in the mud and crushed one of his legs, and he'd been on disability ever since. Now his brother worked at the dump. In fact, he was the supervisor there, having quit school to take on the position. His father sat at home all day and drank himself silly. Vehemently, Frankie confided that he was not about to follow in their footsteps. He had a part-time job at a 7-Eleven and was putting aside money to buy a car. As soon as he had it, he was taking off, to start fresh somewhere.

He stated only the facts, and I was left to ponder the emotions that he must have experienced along with each of these ordeals. I envisioned his parents, toothless and drunk, shouting and hurling things at each other while Frankie and his brother looked on in fright. I saw him standing over his mother's corpse, wondering if her slight smile signified that she was glad to have escaped it all, promising himself that for her sake, if nothing else, he would find a way to escape as well. I saw his father, supine on a couch, a drink on the floor beside him, watching the TV (would they have one?), sliding his eyes from the set to Frankie, mumbling something like "Hang out the laundry, asshole," or "Get dinner going, asshole."

Had I not seen the house, I don't think I would have believed such an improbable story, but as I had, there was no reason to doubt him. I thought of Sherwood Anderson's "Queer," from his *Winesburg, Ohio.* We had read the short story in English the year before, and our teacher had said that Anderson's character, Elmer Cowley, could not shake his crass beginnings, that what Anderson was suggesting, with that ending particularly, was that Elmer's life would be quite the same wherever he went, that always he would carry his "differences" along with him; he would always be "queer" no matter where he escaped to. I remembered that Sharon had defended Elmer, arguing that Anderson had meant to suggest that he *would* change his life. As evidence, she brought in some biographical material on Anderson, who had once been a successful but unhappy businessman. According to the author, he just got up one day, left his thriving business behind him, walked to another town, and started a new life, as a writer.

I hadn't given it much thought at the time, but now I hoped with all my heart that Mrs. Rosen was wrong and that Sharon was right.

The following week was much too cold in my opinion for a dog as old as Surge to be hiking, so I came up with an alternative strategy. I simply left a note on Frankie's locker saying that I had half of the money that I still owed and would he mind coming over to get it before I spent it on something else. Of course he came. He brought a soiled ball for Surge, and they had quite a noisy game of catch in the living room, leaving marks on the walls which I would later have to clean off.

Mom was out that day Christmas shopping with Ida and some woman from her support group, so we had the house to ourselves. I made him lunch, which he ate sitting sideways in his chair so that he could watch Surge gnaw his rawhide bone, and then, when he seemed about to take his leave,

I asked whether he would mind giving me his opinion on something I had got in the mail from a friend the day before. Yes, this time Sharon had sent her correspondence to me. As if she thought I might be too stupid to realize that I should share it with Terri, she sent an extra copy with *For Terri* scrawled at the top. Like the last one, it was unsigned and no note was enclosed.

I read the pages over Frankie's shoulder:

Letter written by asylum inmate Geraldine Love to her father three months after the murder of Geoffrey Bates:

Dear Daddy,

I know you haven't come because you don't believe me, so I'm going to tell you one more time. Please listen.

The evening before it happened, I got this call. I answered, "Kleeman's Cleaners, How can I help you?" like I always did, and the man at the other end laughed, a horrible laugh, Daddy. He said, "It's me who's going to help you." And I said, "Oh, yeah, how's that?" And he whispered, "I'm going to help you put an end to it all, to your miserable existence, tomorrow night."

I should have called the police, but I kept thinking, It's probably someone who was just dialing randomly, calling lots of people and saying the same thing. The next day I told Mr. Kleeman, and he said that the only difference between me and the other people this nut might have called was that by answering the phone that way, I had let the nut know where to find me. He said there was no sense calling the police because they always got people complaining about crank calls and would just say not to worry about it. But he showed me where he kept his gun, just in case.

He left then, and I was okay at first. We didn't have much business, but the few people who did come in were familiar to me. But you'll recall that the other stores at the strip mall closed at 9, and since we closed at 9:30, I began to get really nervous that last half hour. I kept pacing back and forth between the window and the drawer where the gun was. Finally, I got it out and put it in my smock pocket. I had it cocked, all ready to go.

Please, Daddy, try to understand. Someone had threatened to kill me. You can't imagine what that kind of thing does to your mind. I should have closed up. I should have called Mr. Kleeman and told him I was leaving early. But you know how I am, Daddy. I hate to make waves.

At 9:17 I went to the register to count out the money. My hands were quaking, and I kept losing my place. I heard a car pull up, but I kept counting, trying to stay composed. I told myself that it must be Mr. Kleeman, that he'd realized how scared I was, but of course it wasn't him.

The man just stood there, Daddy. If he'd said, "Hi, I came to pick up my laundry," anything . . .

But he just stood there. I was so sure it was him. I didn't have any doubts. I was scared for my life! I shot.

He fell between two machines, so that only his feet were sticking out. I put down the gun and was moving to the phone to call the police when I noticed that he had a ticket stub in his hand. I recognized the numbers as belonging to a suit that I'd cleaned earlier. Then the door opened again.

I had my back to it, and I didn't turn around. I was frozen, paralyzed. "I'm here," he said.

He came forward slowly—I heard his footsteps on the tile—and then he must have noticed the dead man between the machines because he stopped and made a noise, a kind of growl. There was a long, horrible moment of silence, and then I heard his footsteps retreating.

That's the truth, Daddy. That's what I live with, all day in my thoughts and all night in my dreams. "I'm here," I hear, over and over. And the man who said it is loose somewhere, stalking other young women for all I know. And I'm here, locked up like a criminal.

I hope you'll come to see me, Daddy. I'm so alone.

Love,
Geraldine

He put the pages down and stared at me. "What the hell kind of a letter is that?" he asked.

"Well, you'd have to know Sharon," I began. "She's not like the other girls at school. She's not like anyone."

"What the hell are you talking about?"

As Frankie had never asked me a question about myself, I took this to be a close cousin and lavished my response with detail; I told him all about Sharon and Terri and me back in the old days, all about Sharon's dedication to her investigations. In short, I took the opportunity, via my connection to

Sharon, to make myself sound interesting. And Frankie, if not exactly spellbound, did appear to be mildly intrigued. It might have gone the other way; I had taken a risk by showing him the typed pages. He might have held her correspondence up as a warning to me, about what can happen when you carry a gun. But he didn't. He was much more concerned with determining whether Sharon had made the letter up or had actually come upon it somehow. ("Where the hell did she get it?" were his exact words, I think.) I showed him her previous correspondence then, the statement she had sent to Terri. He read it carefully.

"She was that fattish girl with the raincoat, right?"

He shook his head, as if to say, Funny what you might learn about fat girls who wear raincoats. "Geraldine Love," he muttered. "Sounds like a made-up name. Why don't you just ask her?"

I explained why I couldn't, which of course necessitated a detailed account of everything that had happened to Terri and Sharon and me in the first weeks that followed the killings. When he indicated that he had some interest in that day itself ("Cool," he said when I first mentioned it), I realized I had another subject on which I was well versed to speak to him.

He looked at me while I spoke, and not from the corner of one eye and with his head tilted back like he usually did. I had the feeling that he was seeing me for the first time. His life being what it was, it was likely that he seldom tried to imagine what life must be like for other people. I imagined that we would be close now, that in the days to come, we would tell each other everything—as Terri and Sharon and I had once done. To test my hunch, I described something of the emotions that I had experienced and was still experiencing as a result of that one day. But I could see that he was not as interested in my recurrent nightmares and my struggles to cling to my sanity as he was in the facts. He had heard the story from Tom Heely, he said, who had heard it from someone else. As in the children's game of telephone, it had reached his ears distorted, with some things thrown in that hadn't actually occurred. In his version, which could only have come, albeit indirectly, from Sharon herself,

111

Sharon had seen the killer's gun aimed at Bev and had tried to throw herself on top of her.

I set him straight. Then, in one final attempt to get him to focus on me, on who I was aside from that one day, I took my narrative back one day in time, so that I could include my first encounter with Goliath. At this point his gaze drifted off toward Surge. He nodded, as if to indicate that he was still listening, but he patted his leg simultaneously, and Surge came to him.

I quit mid-sentence and offered, instead, to make him a cup of coffee before he left.

11

The children painted with relish, and with a great deal of noise as well, though the result of their labors was a terrible thing to see. Ida had encouraged them to mix their own colors, and most of them had gotten carried away. Their skies were muddy and punctuated by missed spots, patches of brown cardboard that looked like debris flying across the firmament. Their mountains were worse, some red and volcanic-looking, some blurred at the edges, some snow-capped with a thick white that dribbled down the cardboard into the more temperate zones.

When she wasn't in the back with the painters and me, Ida was in the front by the tables, where Flo and the younger children were laying out the animals and flowers and clouds they had been working on for the past months. The errors that had for so long evaded Ida caught her eye now, and she extracted the worst of the projects and set them before Flo, whose task it was to patch them up. The children, who had been led to believe their projects were perfection itself, were no more surprised by this change of attitude than Flo and I.

On the way home, Ida spoke not a word to me, and I was left to consider my own bleak thoughts. Frankie and I were spending quite a lot of time together, but Surge was always at the center of it. The poor old dog, who had at first reacted to Frankie's affections with such enthusiasm, was showing his true colors now. It had been a charade, apparently, and he could not keep it up. Now when Frankie arrived, Surge stood just long enough to wag his tail in greeting and then settled himself again on his rug. And Frankie, who feared the wintry weather was responsible, spent most of our time together cataloguing the changes that spring would bring while the object of his apprehension drifted off to sleep.

For the most part I was content to sit on the edge of my bed and observe the two of them, loving Frankie for his tenderness. But there were times when, watching Frankie stroke Surge's back or rub his palm on Surge's nose, I thought I would explode with jealousy. Once my craving for his touch got so bad that I challenged him to a game of arm wrestling. He looked at me as if I were crazy, then got up and moved the lamp back on my night table. We locked hands, joined elbows, looked into each other's eyes. But before I could make my face lovable, kissable, my arm was down and Frankie was back at Surge's side again.

I didn't know that Ida intended to visit with Mom until we pulled into the driveway and Ida turned off the ignition. Before I could even collect my school books from the back seat, Ida was up the walkway and rapping on the door. I was just heading up the walk myself when Mom appeared in the doorway. I saw her look go from surprise, as Ida always called first when she was coming, to concern—a reaction, I suppose, to Ida's face. She pulled Ida in and was about to close the door when she noticed me.

I followed them into the kitchen where Ida, who was still wearing her coat, immediately began to pace. Mom offered her a glass of wine, but Ida didn't seem to hear her. "What?" Mom asked. "What? Tell me, Ida."

"It's Charles," Ida said, wringing her hands. Her voice was so low that it sounded more like a growl than a reply. She reminded me of those tigers that you see pacing in the zoo, the ones that cannot be distracted from the reality of their imprisonment.

"What?" Mom asked. "What did he do to you?"

"He invited another couple," Ida said flatly.

"What? To go on the boat?"

"He said it would be more fun that way, people to share our time with and so forth."

Mom's lips moved, groping for an appropriate response. "Oh, Ida, that's not the end of the world," she said at last. "You're still going. That's the important thing. It doesn't mean that he doesn't care about you."

Ida's expression did not alter, nor did she quit pacing. I

114

stood in the corner of the room clutching my books to my chest, longing for my bedroom but afraid to draw attention to myself by making any sudden movements. "Who's the other couple?" Mom asked weakly.

"Ed."

"Ed!" Mom laughed bitterly.

"Ed and some woman he's apparently been seeing." Mom pulled out a chair and slowly sank into it, her expression now as dazed as Ida's. "Why didn't you tell me?"

"I didn't know," Ida said. She reached the counter and turned sharply. "Until last night."

Mom turned towards me, wide-eyed, then away again.

Ida shook her head. "I can't go. I won't."

"Don't be ridiculous," Mom said. Her tone was testy. "You like Ed. I'm sure his friend is very nice. You've been looking forward to this trip for weeks. You can't cancel it on my account."

"I can't do this to you."

Mom lifted herself from the chair and went to the refrigerator, nearly colliding with Ida on her way. She extracted a half-empty bottle of Zinfandel and sank into her chair again, then realized that she had forgotten to get a glass and looked beseechingly in my direction. I put my books down quickly and got out two glasses. Mom filled them, holding one out for Ida.

Ida stopped to stare at it, greedily, I thought, but then she shook her head. "Oh, come on," Mom said with forced cheerfulness. "It's no big deal. Charles is right. You *do* make mountains out of molehills sometimes. Stop that damn pacing, would you? You're driving me crazy." She furrowed her brows. "Actually, why would Ed want to go? He has no sailing experience."

"That's why he wants to go," Ida mumbled.

"What? Speak up, damn it."

"Charles says he wants to come because of some book he's writing. About pirates. He wants the experience on a boat so that he can get it right."

"And Charles just said yes? After he promised you that it would just be the two of you?"

"He said he just mentioned it to him, casually, and Ed got so excited about the idea of coming along—"

"Ed excited? That's a laugh."

"—And Charles didn't know how to tell him that it was supposed to be a sort of second honeymoon."

Mom made a fist and brought it down on the table. "Well, Ed's entitled to a life, I suppose, and you're certainly entitled to one too. It's not the end of the world. What you and Charles do as a couple has nothing to do with our friendship."

She stopped talking to gulp down some wine, then put her head down on the table and began to sob. Ida stood behind her with her hands held up uncertainly. Eventually, she lowered them onto Mom's shoulders and began to massage. Mom lifted her head and attempted a laugh. "Ida, Ida, Ida. Do you really imagine that I still entertain the thought that we might get back together after all this time? Of course it hurts! But there's nothing to be done about it. Your not going won't change a thing."

Can I help? I wrote, once Ida had gone. Mom was still at the table, resting her head on it again. I held my note sideways so that she could read it, but she only shook her head.

I found a jar of tomato sauce in the pantry and put some water on to boil for elbow macaroni. The phone rang, but Mom didn't answer it. *Don't you have Bingo tonight?* I wrote. She shrugged. I lowered my head to stare into her eyes, but she wouldn't look at me. There were strands of hair clinging to her face. When I latched one with my fingernail and pulled it away, she shook her head in warning.

We had our dinner in total silence, with Mom staring at the wall beyond me and stabbing one strand of macaroni at a time. I had homework to do, but I was reluctant to leave her in her present state. The phone rang again, but she still didn't answer. I pushed my plate aside, got my pad, and began my confession. *I knew about it,* I wrote. *But I couldn't bring myself to tell you, in part because I didn't want to hurt you and in part because I didn't think, and still don't, that the relationship was/is serious.*

I kept glancing up at her as I wrote, but she was still staring at the wall, seemingly unaware of the fact that I was writing a note for her. Suddenly she jumped up, dashed to the phone, and dialed.

"Mom," she said, clearing her throat, "listen. Ginny and I aren't coming down for Christmas. . . .

"No, no, we have the money. It's not that . . . No, not that either . . . I'm simply not up to it, Mom . . . No, that isn't what I meant . . . No, don't go getting—"

I considered this turn of events. On the one hand, I was greatly relieved. Mom and I had spent our last Christmas vacation going with Grandma to flea markets each day and eating in crowded cafeterias at night. In the late afternoons, while Grandma napped, Mom and I had gone to the pool, where we were the youngest people and the only ones to venture into the water. This year would have been even worse. Killing tourists in Florida had become some kind of a game, and I had already informed Mom that I wasn't leaving the condo, that I would take no responsibility for her if she was inclined to do so. Furthermore, the idea of sitting on an airplane among strangers and taking a cab with a driver who would undoubtedly be carrying a gun had already cost me several sleepless nights.

They were still on the phone; Mom was coming clean now. I put my plate in the sink, took the confession I'd begun, and went to my room. I crumpled up the note and got out my trampoline, hoping it would facilitate my thought processes. The problem was that I'd already told Frankie that we would be away, and he was more than excited about the prospect of having Surge all to himself for ten days. He'd already told his father, and after an argument—relatively painless, Frankie said—his father agreed to let Surge sleep in the house next to the wood stove.

Frankie had plans. He had taken some of the money that he was saving for his car and bought Surge some presents for Christmas morning, rawhide bones and balls and squeaky toys. ("Will you have a tree then?" I'd asked him. "No, this is gonna be a private affair," he'd said.)

Of course, I could still have him take Surge, but it wouldn't be quite the same. I had told him several times that he would be doing us a tremendous favor. I had called a kennel and ascertained that it would cost $100 to board a dog Surge's size for ten days. Then I had written a note to Mom informing her of this astronomical fee and asking whether we could at least offer Frankie $50 for his trouble. It had taken several notes more, but I had finally got her to agree.

I did not, however, intend to pay him; I didn't believe he would accept the money. What I wanted to do was to go to the mall with Mom's fifty and whatever I had left after paying off the gun, and buy him a Christmas present, one nice outfit that would fit him properly. I had come across Frankie's double in an Abraham & Straus advertisement in the magazine section of *The New York Times* the week before. In the picture, his double perched on the edge of a plush-looking dark green sofa with four smartly dressed, attractive female models—one of whom resembled me, I thought. His double wore off-white jeans and a gray V-necked short-sleeved T-shirt. He even sat like Frankie, with his knees spread apart and his hands folded in between. The resemblance was striking. The only differences were that his double's hair was squeaky clean, and that Frankie was a loner, except in the cafeteria where he was surrounded not by girls, but by other apparent losers.

I planned to enclose the ad along with his gift. I imagined that he might be confused at first, maybe even insulted. However, I imagined too that when he tried on the pants and the shirt and looked in the mirror (would he have one?), he would see how much he resembled the model in the picture and see, as well, my vision for him, for his future, that *I*, at least, realized that he was no Elmer Cowley, that I believed him capable of escaping the abject circumstances of his life.

It did not stop there. I had hopes that the day would come when he would yet allow me to tutor him. I had offered once, but he had said, "I *get* C's, Jarrell. What the hell is the matter with you?"

I imagined that one day I would read poetry to him the way Sharon had read it to Terri and me, that we would eventually embark on lengthy discussions of literature and philosophy (God, did I miss my former life), that he would excel in his senior year and ultimately would be offered a scholarship to some small school in Boston.

And that was only the beginning. I imagined late night dinners in candle-lit cafés, afternoon walks on the Commons. His love for me, I imagined, would enable me to conquer my fears and enjoy such public places again. There would be rendezvous in his dorm, rendezvous in mine, marriage, successful careers, checks sent to his father to help him to rehabilitate, children (my smile, his eyes and shapely brows), a small brick house with a white picket fence and a pond in the back yard for Surge.

Mom and I *had* to go to Florida. A gift of such import could not be given if it were clear that he was taking Surge merely for his own amusement.

I heard Mom's whining cease and then her footsteps coming down the hall. Her bedroom door opened and closed, and then I heard her voice again, on the phone in there.

She was on quite long, a half hour maybe. I could hear nothing of what she actually said, but as her tone seemed persuasive, I concluded she must be talking to Ida, still trying to get her to go. Then there was silence, so that I supposed she had finished her call and was resting on her bed. Thinking she might be calm enough now to be sensible, I jumped off my trampoline, got my pad and pencil, and opened my door.

She was just coming out of her room, which was across from mine, and we nearly collided. She had washed her face and pulled her hair back into a ponytail. "Ginny!" she said, smiling.

I need to talk to you, I wrote, *about Florida.*

"Don't worry about Florida. We're not going. I already told Grandma."

I went to write again, but she slipped my pencil out from between my fingers and stuck it in the pocket of her jeans. Then she took my arm and led me back into my room, closing the door behind her. "You, young lady," she declared cheerfully, "are going someplace very special for Christmas."

I looked with longing at my pencil, but she covered it with her hand. Then her eyes hardened, and I realized all at once that what I had taken for cheerfulness a moment before was actually an attempt to conceal an emotion far more bizarre.

119

"Your father has agreed that it would be a wonderful experience for you to go along with him and his friend and the Newets on this sailing trip," she said.

My mouth dropped open, and I might have voiced my revulsion aloud if she had not, just then, lifted a finger and thrust it at my collar bone just hard enough to cause me to fall back onto the bed.

"It's all arranged," she went on. "Your father says you've been like a stranger with him lately. In fact, he tells me he hasn't even seen you since Thanksgiving. This will give you a chance to patch things up. You'll be chartering a plane . . . nice to have money, isn't it? . . . and flying to North Carolina. From there, you'll be taking a boat to some little island where nobody lives. So you see, you won't have to worry about people carrying guns and shooting tourists and that kind of thing.

"So, where was I? Oh yes, this little island you're going to. You'll be pitching a tent there for a few nights and then sailing back again. You're a very lucky girl, and I'm a lucky woman," she stated, and then, in an incredibly loud voice, "BECAUSE I'M GOING TO SPEND CHRISTMAS ALL ALONE, ALL DAY LONG IN BED, SLEEPING AND READING AND READING AND SLEEPING AND THINKING OVER MY LIFE. IN FACT, YOU CAN TELL THAT SLOPPY YOUNG MAN THAT YOU'VE BEEN HANGING AROUND WITH THAT HE CAN STILL COME AND GET SURGE AND I'll STILL PAY HIM THE $50 OR WHATEVER IT IS. BECAUSE I DON'T WANT TO HAVE TO GO OUT AND TIE SURGE UP AND THEN GO OUT AND GET HIM AND BRING HIM IN WITH HIS FEET ALL MUDDY."

She stopped to take a deep breath. "AND WHETHER YOU TALK OR DON'T TALK WILL BE YOUR FATHER'S CONCERN FOR ONE GLORIOUS WEEK. AND WHETHER YOU DECIDE TO GO INTO THERAPY OR TO SPEND THE REST OF YOUR LIFE CLINGING TO YOUR ANGER . . . YES, THAT'S RIGHT, LITTLE GIRL. DON'T MAKE THOSE EYES AT ME. I TALKED ALL ABOUT IT TO MY TAI CHI TEACHER, AND HE EXPLAINED ALL ABOUT HOW YOUR ANGER CAN CRE-

ATE KARMIC TIES WHICH IN TURN CREATE SIMILAR SITUATIONS . . ."

She lowered her voice a little. "And you know what? When you come home, I'm going to be a new woman. Yes, that's right. Just like a butterfly crawling out of a cocoon. I'm going to beat my wings and take flight. MY LIFE IS GOING TO BEGIN AGAIN!"

12

Dear Sharon,

Who do you think you are, anyway?

Do you realize what it took for Terri and me to keep from getting in touch with you those first months? We've fallen apart, our little group. Terri and I don't even speak to each other anymore. I suspect she has turned to drink. Can you even imagine that, Sharon? Little, shy, peaceful, intelligent Terri coming into school everyday half-cocked? Red-eyed? Slurring her way through her responses in class? Walking through the halls with her head dangling? Sitting alone in the cafeteria, pretending to be reading, but never as much as turning a page?

You were the one who insisted we suspend all contact, and then you go and break your own rules, although in the most bizarre way imaginable. What were those "documents" supposed to be? What were we supposed to make of them? Did you actually acquire them? And if so, how? Or did you simply make them up for the sake of some wild experiment meant to drive us even further into our respective infernos? What is going on in your mind? If your object was to dissuade us from communication, then why did you bother to send them in the first place? You must have realized that with Terri and me being curious by nature, they would have the opposite effect.

Anyway, it is on the assumption that your "documents" were actually an appeal, whether conscious or not, that I am writing. If I am wrong, if either you or your therapist feel that this letter may have the potential to do you further psychological damage, please tear it up this instant.

(The above line of space represents a change in tone, in attitude.)

You won't believe it, but I am writing to you from somewhere out in the middle of the sea—well, not quite the middle, actually we're in the sound, on a sailboat. I am here with my father and Goliath. You see, I was right; he was seeing her. Ida and Charles Newet, who you met once or twice at our house, are with us too.

I should mention that I've been working for Ida, at the day-care center for a total of fifteen hours a week. I wish I could tell you why I took the job and what it has enabled me to acquire, but it would be remiss of me to specify in a letter. Let's just say that after months of horrifying dreams by night and even more horrifying fantasies by day—involving everyone from the mailman to the president at the bank where I go to cash my paycheck—I have finally achieved a feeling of relative security.

Our boat is a nineteen-foot sloop. It sleeps only two, but as we intend to reach our destination, a small uninhabited island off the North Carolina coast, by nightfall, this is not a concern. The cabin is small, but the weather is lovely, sunny skies and about 70 degrees, and we are all above deck. Dad and Goliath and the Newets are drinking beer in the cockpit, and I am lying on the bow. Except for the lapping of water, it is so quiet that I can hear Goliath when she sighs, which is often.

The boat has a swing centerboard, and if I understood the man from whom we chartered it correctly, if we run aground, we only need to pull up the centerboard, get out, and give the boat a little push to get her going again. I am on the lookout for sharks, which the man said are sometimes seen in these waters. So far I have seen only tiny flying fish.

Since Ida is Mom's best friend, she was reluctant to acquaint herself with Goliath, but in fact they seem to be hitting it off quite well. Goliath was once a dancer and now teaches yoga to business people, Charles and his staff among them. She has quite a body, which was, I thought initially, what must have attracted my father to her. She is all legs and breasts, with shoulders that are quite broad. She laughs often, opening her mouth wide and throwing her head back. Actually, she's rather comical, and I have to admit that I am beginning to like her myself.

For instance, earlier, when there was a lull in their conversation, Goliath said, "I read this incredible thing in Ann Landers sometime back." Her voice is raspy, loud, and deep for a woman. In fact, between that and her incredible height, there is a manishness about her, as if she is the embodiment of both sexes equally.

"This unemployed man was having an affair, at his house, in the afternoons while his wife was at work. Well, one day he and his mistress had concluded their business and the mistress was dressing and getting ready to leave and he was still lying in bed, naked, watching her, when all of a sudden the wife comes home unexpectedly. But he's one of those guys who's good on his feet," ("I thought he was lying down," goofy Charles interrupted.) "so he smiles when his wife comes into the room and introduces her to his mistress who he says is a massage therapist.

"Since he's got a bad back and because he's such a convincing liar, and maybe because she's stupid too, the wife believes *him! She even asks for an appointment for herself, because she wakes up with a kink in her neck every morning, and also she's got tennis elbow." ("You're embellishing," my father said here. "I read that one too.")*

"So, anyway, the mistress is the one who wrote to Ann. Now that she's been giving the wife massages on a regular basis, and getting paid for it, what she wants to know is not how she can get out of this outrageous situation, but whether or not she can get into trouble for practicing without a license!"

I laughed, and Goliath winked at me. The point, however, is that the things that Goliath comes up with are always impersonal, and after listening these past months to Mom and Ida, who are always talking about their feelings, it's refreshing. I imagine my father thinks so too.

Oh, I should mention that I don't talk at all anymore—except to one new friend who I will tell you about another time. I have become an avid listener, and when I have something to say, which is seldom, I write it on this little pad I carry and show it to whomever it is intended for.

Well, Sharon, have a merry Christmas. I'm sorry you can't be here with me. I am sure there are a number of things worth investigating on this island. Without you to guide me, I will probably miss half of them.

Much Love,
G.J.

13

Dear Frankie,

I took your advice and wrote a letter to Sharon. Of course I won't be able to mail it to her until we get back to the mainland. We will be staying in a hotel in New Bern for two nights before we fly back to New York, so she should receive it before I return. My hope is that by the time you come by to bring Surge home, I will have had a full account concerning her acquisition of the "documents."

But that is not what I really want to talk to you about.

I am very embarrassed by my reaction to your "Christmas gift." You see, you hadn't told me that your brother had concluded his dealings, and so when you handed me a shoe box wrapped in the funnies and tied with a piece of yellow yarn, naturally I thought it was a real gift, something you had gone out and chosen for me. Given the fact that I know very well that you are saving every penny you make for your car, I was deeply touched. That's why I threw my arms around you and kissed you like that. Then, when you pushed me away, naturally I was confused. And when you said, "It's only the ____, Jarrell", in that tone. . . . Well, I was deeply hurt. That's why I called you that. I had promised myself that I would never call you that again, especially after I learned that your father does. But I was hurt and full of conflicting emotions, and it just came out. I'm so very sorry.

You must understand that there were some other things going on too. I mean, you can imagine how I felt, having just learned that I am an affliction to my very own mother. And I overheard enough of her telephone conversation with my father to know that he had to be begged to take me along. I know you can relate to this. I know you know what it's like to be unwanted.

Now that I've had some time to think about it, I know too, even if you may not yet be ready to admit it to yourself, that you have at least some feeling for me. Otherwise, why would you have taken the time and the trouble to wrap the ____ like that? It must have taken some effort, given the fact that your hand was all bandaged up. How did you cut your hand, Frankie? Why were you so annoyed when I asked about it?

And let me say a word too about the gift that I gave you, which you will have opened by the time you read this. The A&S ad I enclosed, I fear after the way we parted company, may seem to you to be some kind of an affront, even the outfit may. But that is just the opposite of what I intended. I only wanted you to know that I believe in you, that I believe in your future.

I look forward to seeing you next week.

Sincerely,
G.J.

14

Dear Sharon,

You won't believe what's happened since I last wrote to you . . . yesterday? Yes, it must have been, although it seems more like last week.

I wrote your letter and one other and then I went down into the galley to help Ida, who was making sandwiches. As we were working, Goliath appeared and said, "Ida! What are you doing making sandwiches? You're the captain!"

You see, Ida had some sailing lessons a while back, some courses and then a week or so of hands-on. She had to show the various certificates that she'd earned to the man at the marina in order for us to charter the boat. She was the only one who was qualified to sign for it. The man went out with us for a few hours, to familiarize Ida with this particular craft. He reviewed the nautical charts with her, and then he had her do some tacks and turns, etc. When he was satisfied, we sailed him back to the marina and took off on our own.

As soon as we were underway though, it was Charles who took over. Ida didn't seem to mind, really; like Terri, she's rather submissive by nature. But when Goliath came down and said that about Ida being the captain, Ida sat down, and I realized that it had been bothering her all along.

She began to cry, not hard, but a few sniffles, and with her head turned to the side so that Goliath wouldn't notice. But of course Goliath did, and then she came and sat next to her, and with a genuine look of concern on her face, wrapped her long arms around her. "Sweetheart," she said, "you've got to learn to stand up for yourself. It's a dog-eat-dog world out there. If you don't look out for yourself, who's going to?"

Well, to make a long story short, Ida broke down and confided in her. She told her all about how Charles has been emotionally abusive to her over the last several months and how she doesn't know what it is that caused him, a loving husband for twenty-one years, to change. She showed Goliath this little tattoo she got back in October right behind her ear, a little red heart with an "I" in the middle of it that's supposed to remind her to love herself even when Charles seems not to. And as proof that Charles seems not to most of the time, she confessed that Charles still hasn't seen the thing, which happens to be in the very place that he had once liked most to kiss when their lovemaking was through.

Well, Goliath was wonderful, holding her and rocking her as if Ida were a little girl. Naturally, that only brought on more tears, more confessions. (You may be wondering how this could all have taken place in front of me, but if you remember from my first letter, I am a non-talker now. The fact is, when you stop talking, people, adults at least, seem to forget that you are present and will often carry on just as though you weren't.)

Goliath rocked and Ida, between sniffles, catalogued the various campaigns, in addition to the tattoo, that she has undertaken in recent times in order to rise above Charles's indifference. She has been to rebirthing classes, along with my mother, where, apparently, the self you don't like attempts to deliver a self you do. She has gone for "skipping therapy" (yes, you read it right), the premise of which is that since our happiest years were those in which we were uninhibited enough to skip in public places (ages three? four?), a return to skipping, after hours, on our high school track, will ultimately resuscitate the child within. The list goes on: Shiatsu, Tui Na, channeling, and, most recently, a winter solstice workshop in which the return of the lengthening light of the sun, and thus hope, is celebrated. "Nothing's helped," Ida lamented.

Goliath went to the sink, wet a dishcloth, and gently wiped the tears from Ida's face. "Now we'll try something new," she declared. "It's called Take Charge Therapy."

Just then, as if on cue, Charles called down, "Aren't you girls done with those sandwiches yet?"

Foolish Ida, who only a moment before had nodded determinedly in response to Goliath's suggestion, rose from her seat and moved toward the sandwich tray. Goliath and I both saw what was about to happen and beat her there. Ida looked at us and laughed, and when we were all up in the cockpit again, she said, "Charles, I'd like to take over for a while if you don't mind."

Charles only stared at first, but then Goliath gave him a look and he smiled and said, "Sure, go ahead." He took a sandwich and got another beer from the cooler. After he finished eating, he leaned back against the cushions and went to sleep.

Ida was at the helm a good four hours, checking the chart occasionally and giving the rest of us orders when it was time to tack. She smiled the entire time, so I knew that Goliath had done her a world of good.

We spotted land, finally: our little island off in the distance. Everyone stood up to look, including Charles. "I'll take over now," he said. Goliath opened her mouth to protest, but Ida caught her eye and gestured with her hand as if to say, It's okay now, I've had my moment in the sun and I'm satisfied.

As we maneuvered through the shoals, Charles explained that there was once a small settlement on the island, but the shifting shoals eventually rendered its small port inaccessible to all but the shallowest-drafted boats. Though visitors still come to the island now and then, to fish or gather shells, there have been no residents for nearly fifty years. The Rangers come by only when a major storm is threatening, to make sure that no one is marooned there.

Charles decided to make his approach toward the southern end, which was nearest, but Ida, who had the chart, said, "Charles, I think we should head north for bit, to where the port once was."

"That'll take longer," Charles replied. "It's getting late. We'll need time to set up the tents before it gets dark."

His words were gentle, but I happened to glance at him as he was saying them and I saw that there was much more communicated in the look he shot at her than his tone implied. Ida's eyes moistened slightly behind her glasses. She looked to Goliath for help, but she was busy helping my father taking down the sails.

We came in over the salt marsh, a dense mat of various grasses that smelled like rotten eggs. It thinned as we got closer to the beach and I was able to see a small blue crab scuttling away from us. I saw too a pale-colored whelk, and when it moved, I realized that it was the property of a hermit crab. When we were close enough, we all climbed over the gunwale and began to pull in the boat. It didn't take as much of an effort as you might think, because the tide was coming in and all but pushed us to the beach. Once there, of course, it was somewhat more difficult. Charles and Dad got back in the boat and, in their effort to lighten it as much as possible, went below and retrieved our supplies. Then they passed them one by one to Goliath who passed them to me, and I passed them on to Ida who piled them on the sand. Then the men got out and we all pushed again, and in the end we managed to get the boat about three-quarters out of the water and onto the beach. Then Charles ordered us each to take something and head inland.

"Shouldn't we put the anchor down first?" Ida asked.

"What for?" Charles replied. "The boat's not going anywhere with the tide coming in like this."

"Well, we can't leave the boat overnight without an anchor," Ida said.

"I looked at the anchor earlier. I didn't like the looks of it," Charles answered. "One of the flukes doesn't pivot the way it should. I think we're better off tying up for the night."

Ida looked around. "To what, Charles?"

"Those trees there," he said, indicating the maritime forest some fifty feet back from the beach.

"We don't have a line that long," Ida said.

"We have several lines. We'll tie them together."

"Fine. Let's do that."

"We'll do it later, Ida, after we've set up camp."

"Why can't we just do it now?"

"Because, Ida, we don't have enough lantern light to be pitching tents in the dark. Let's get the tents pitched and then we'll come back and do whatever we have to do to secure the boat."

They stared at each other, with the rest of us watching them. I'm sure Goliath would have defended Ida, for the sake of principle if nothing else, but she was holding her nose against the terrible smell with one hand and slapping the mosquitoes that landed on her bare legs with the other. When Charles picked up his duffel bag and one of the tents and headed off, Goliath gathered up our sleeping bags, which were all strapped together, and immediately began to follow.

I was anxious to get out of there myself, so I picked up the second tent and started off behind them. When I reached the trees, I looked back and saw Ida and Dad coming up with the cooler, a comical sight because Dad is so much taller and his end was higher, while Ida, who was huffing and puffing, had most of the weight.

The forest was dense and dark, but we got through it and came to a sandy knoll from which we could see a line of cottages in the distance. From what Charles had said, I had expected them to be in various stages of disintegration; but, in fact, though some were run-down (broken windows, missing roof tiles) there were a few that looked as if their owners might just have gone out for the day. One even had a perfectly solid picket fence all around it, and that was the one that Goliath was looking at when she exclaimed, "How cute! Why, we don't need the tents at all. We can sleep in there."

"But Rita," Ida protested. "That's trespassing!"

Goliath turned to look at her, her greenish eyes twinkling with delight. "We're not going to be doing any harm. No one lives here. No one is ever going to live here. What's the difference?"

Dad, who had been quiet all day, said, "It may not be structurally sound."

"Then again it may," Goliath said. "Let's find out."

"It would save us a lot of time," Charles offered, smiling at Goliath.

"Time," Ida mumbled, but when the others glanced at her, she just shook her head.

Ida and I sat down on the cooler while Dad, Goliath, and Charles went to look. They got in with no difficulty; the door wasn't even locked. A moment later a window opened, and Goliath stuck her head out. "It's furnished!" she squealed, and disappeared again. Then the door opened and Charles yelled, "It's sound, come on."

It was more than sound, Sharon. It was charming and not nearly as dirty as you might imagine. "Maybe the park rangers are still keeping it up after all," Charles said. "Or maybe some fishermen who come here every year," Goliath suggested.

There were three small bedrooms, with two cots apiece, a kitchen with a coal-burning stove, and a small living room with four club chairs, all with broken springs. We staked out our rooms and spread our sleeping bags out on the cots. Ida found a broom and began sweeping while Goliath took the cushions from the living room chairs outside and beat them against the side of the house. I gathered all the floor runners and shook them out in the little sandy yard. In the meantime, Dad and Charles took a lantern and set out to get the rest of our supplies from the beach and to tie up the boat.

Time passed and it got dark, and still they weren't back. We couldn't start dinner because the hibachi was at the boat. Thinking that maybe something had happened to their lantern, in which case *they might need help finding their way, Ida suggested that we gather some branches and make a fire in the yard. Once we got it burning, Goliath went indoors and got a bag of marshmallows and a bottle of wine.*

They passed the bottle back and forth and Goliath tried her best to keep a conversation going, but Ida responded with monosyllables to her comments about the beauty of our surroundings and kept her gaze set on the direction from which we expected the men to return. When the marshmallows were all gone, she stood up and announced that she was going to look for them. Just then we heard voices in the distance. Goliath laughed and Ida let out a long deep sigh.

It took some time for Charles and Dad to materialize. Goliath called out, "Hurry, would you? We're all starving!" but neither of them answered her. It occurred to me then that it might not be Dad and Charles after all, and I put my hand into my shoulder bag and lay my fingers on the thing which I told you about yesterday. (I fear by now you will have guessed what it is.)

Eventually, I was able to make out the light of their lantern. As they got closer, I saw that Charles had the hibachi in his arms and two of our duffel bags over his shoulders and Dad had the other duffel bags and the carton containing the manuscript he has been working on, as well as his lap top, cigarettes, and several more bottles of wine. As they approached the circle of light generated by our fire, Goliath stood up and exclaimed, "Why, you're all wet!"

"We went for a swim," Dad said flatly. He and Charles looked at each other. There was no pleasure in either of their faces.

"You went swimming when you knew that we were waiting here to get dinner ready?"

"It was necessary," Dad said.

As if they had only come by to say hello, Charles clung to the hibachi and Dad to the carton. They kept looking at each other, their faces ghostly in the firelight. Goliath stood before them with her hands on her hips, waiting for an elaboration. Finally Charles gave her one. "The boat got away," he said.

Ida stepped forward and placed her fingers lightly on Charles's forearm, but he jerked his arm away from her. Dad said, "When we got there, it was just drifting away. It didn't seem that far out. We swam out after it. But it was drifting faster than we could swim. At some point, it became clear that it was an impossible situation."

"We nearly drowned," Charles added.

There was a long moment of silence. Then Goliath threw her head back and laughed. Charles watched her carefully, and eventually a little smile began to quiver on his face too. "We're stranded," Goliath cried. "That's just great!"

Charles realized that her laughter had been sarcastic and hung his head. Ida put her fingers on his arm again. This time he didn't shake her off. "It'll work out," she said. "Tomorrow someone will find the boat and radio to the Coast Guard and they'll come rescue us."

"Maybe," Charles whispered.

"What if the people who find the boat decide to keep it?" Goliath asked. "That could happen too. Or what if no one finds it?"

"Some visitors might come to the island," Ida said. She was trying her best to smile, but her brows were furrowed and her real emotion, I guessed, was terror. "Or someone might sail by and we can flag them down. We'll keep a lookout on the beach."

"And if no one comes by?"

"If we're not back when we're supposed to be, people home will phone the authorities and—"

"Who, Ida?" Goliath snapped. "Charles said your girls are going straight from their skiing vacation back to school. They won't realize we're missing for weeks. Ed has no one and neither do I."

Ida turned to glance at me. "Ginny's mother," she replied, straightening her shoulders.

Dad nodded. Charles smiled. "Let's make the best of it," he declared, turning towards Goliath. "After all, it was because we wanted a little adventure that we planned this trip. Well, this is an adventure."

"Yes, that's true," Goliath said.

Their moods improved after that, so I didn't bother mentioning that Mom and I had parted company on the worst of terms and I doubted if she would care one way or the other if we failed to call her from the mainland on the day we were due back there.

The men went into the house to dry off and change their clothes and Ida, Goliath, and I got the steaks going on the hibachi. We had a super dinner, and afterwards Ida produced from the cooler a chocolate forest cake that she had made at home. Charles opened a second bottle of wine, and claiming that his heart was still racing from his near-death experience, proceeded to drink himself silly. Later he remarked that he was still tense, and Goliath suggested that they go inside and do a little yoga. Charles got up immediately, and giggling like a school boy, waddled indoors. "Yoga, anyone?" Goliath asked. We shook our heads; she shrugged and went in after him.

They had taken one of the lanterns and we could see their silhouettes through the living room window. They were facing each other, a few feet apart. "They look like they're arguing," Ida mumbled.

"I doubt that," Dad said.

Ida turned to look at him, then looked back at the window, but now there was nothing to see. Apparently, they had both dropped to the floor to begin their exercises. "Tell me a little about your book," Ida began. "Charles says he's read some of it and that it's about two female pirates. He said that's why you wanted to come sailing with us, to gain some experience of the sea as part of your research."

Dad, who had been gazing off toward the house, looked at her curiously. Then he sighed and looked at me. "Ginny's going to be helping me with it," he muttered. Since he seemed to be waiting for a confirmation, I nodded. He turned back to Ida then. "She's going to critique some chapters for me. I wasn't going to bring them along, but now that it looks like we might be here longer that we expected, I'm glad I did." He bent his head and rubbed his fingers on his nose. "It was kind of you not to say anything," he said. Ida looked confused. "To Charles," he explained. "About the boat getting away."

Ida threw her hands out. "Well, no sense crying over spilt milk, is there? Besides, I figure he's feeling bad enough without me telling him, 'I told you so'. You know how he is; he holds everything in. He's had a lot on his mind lately, pressure at work, I suppose. He's ripe for one of his anxiety attacks. If he had one here, in front of everyone, he'd be devastated. I think the yoga will help him."

Dad narrowed his eyes into slits, scrutinizing her. Ida responded to his look with an abrupt laugh. "We've changed the subject," she cried. "You were going to tell us about your book."

Dad stuck a cigarette into his mouth and took a stick that was protruding from the fire and used the burning end to light it. He exhaled slowly, with his eyes on the house. "I can't really tell you much about the book because I'm not completely sure where I'm going with it yet, but I can tell you the story on which it's based."

He went on to tell us the entire story then, Sharon, which was fascinating. Basically, it's about Anne Bonny, the woman who married and sailed with the infamous Calico Jack and who was his equal in the atrocities she committed. Dad related many of their adventures, but the one that interests him most, the one that he is focusing on in his book, concerns Anne Bonny's attraction to a sailor whose ship she and Calico Jack captured and who was given the choice of walking the plank or joining the crew. This sailor, who went by the name of M.Read, opted for the latter, and Bonny, who was used to having things her way, set out to seduce him. You can imagine how surprised she was when M. Read was forced to reveal that he was a she! Having been compelled by her parents to dress like a boy in her youth, so that she would appear to be the proper sex to receive her grandmother's inheritance, she had grown accustomed to boys' ways, and when her husband died some years later, she dressed as a male again and escaped to the sea.

As I was curious to see what Dad was doing with this material, when he was done talking about it I dug my pad out of my bag and wrote, Why don't you get me some chapters to look at?

He held my note over the fire to read it. "Now?" he asked. "You can't read by firelight."

I reached into my shoulder bag and removed my headband flashlight. I put it on my head and turned it on. He lifted his hand to shield his eyes from the light and I quickly turned it off again. "Okay," he said, but he still didn't move.

Just then the door opened and Goliath appeared. "Why don't we bring the party indoors?" she called.

So we went inside, Sharon, and Dad gave me his manuscript and I brought it into the bedroom, which is where I am now. But for a time I was too busy listening to the adults in the living room to concentrate on reading.

As soon as Dad and Ida settled in, Goliath suggested that they blow out the lanterns and talk in the dark. At first they just talked about how absolute the dark was, how isolated we were. In spite of the fact that my "companion" is here in my bag at my side, their talk succeeded in frightening me. Then they began to talk about pirates. Ida kept asking why the pirates always seemed to take such delight in their atrocities. "Because the victim is contemptible," Dad said, which got me thinking about all sorts of things which I'd hoped to be able to put out of my mind.

Then Charles asked what I was doing, and when Dad said that I was off reading the manuscript, Charles began to talk about that. "I think you should really play up Bonny's attraction to Read," he said, slurring a little as a result of all the wine he'd drunk. "Let the *reader really feel her obsession. She can't sleep nights. She tosses and turns and gets out of her berth, or whatever it was she would have been sleeping in, and wanders around on the deck wondering how she, being married to the jealous Calico Jack, is going to work this thing out, knowing that she must have Read one way or the other, no matter what the consequences, and unable to think as far ahead as the consequences, just so caught up in the obsession itself that she can't drive her mind to think of anything else. The obsession is the most intriguing part of the story, Ed. If Read makes her confession too soon, before Bonny's obsession has really been fully established, you lose your hook."*

He went on in this vein for some time, and when he was through, Goliath laughed. "You sound like a man obsessed," she hooted. Then she began to talk about dancing, her own obsession. Her voice seemed to come from different places, and I suspect that she was gliding around the room as she spoke. Finally, Ida announced that she was going to bed and asked Charles if he was coming along. No, he said, he wasn't tired. But a moment later Goliath said that she was going to bed, and then Charles said that he might as well go too. Dad is the only one who is still up, sitting in the dark all by himself.

I finished reading the first chapter of his manuscript just before I began this letter. In it he describes Anne Bonny's initial reaction to M. Read. Read keeps apart from the others and Anne finds her far too sullen for her tastes. Still, she is intrigued by Read's looks, which, Dad writes, are "unbearably fragile for a boy on the brink of manhood." The obsession that Charles suggested is not present at all at this point.

But what I am intrigued with, Sharon, are Anne's looks. Dad describes her as being fine-boned, but also broad-shouldered and of remarkable height. And where the true version, as he related it to Ida and me earlier, states that her eyes were blue and her hair black, Dad's Anne has greenish eyes that twinkle when she laughs and reddish hair. He says, in fact, that there is a "manishness" about her, as if she were the "embodiment of both sexes."

My very words, Sharon! (See yesterday's letter.) Do you see what he's doing? He's using Goliath as a model for his Anne Bonny!

I am so confused, Sharon. On the one hand, as far as his relationship with Mom is concerned, this is very good news indeed. On the other, I find this incredibly distasteful. My own father, a criminal of sorts. When an artist hires a model, there is no discrepancy about the role she will play.

Is this the sort of thing that passes for love among adults these days? One person using the other? And how will Goliath feel if and when she reads the manuscript? Surely she'll recognize herself in it; she'll think he believes she's evil. And Sharon, she is anything but. When I think of how sweetly she comforted Ida . . . And can you imagine what virtue she must be endowed with to have bothered to take goofy, drunk Charles (who lost our boat, for God's sake!) into the house to help him relax with yoga?

I'm tired, Sharon. I'm going to end here and go to sleep. If nothing more occurs, then this will be the last you will hear from me until we stranded souls find our way home again. Otherwise, I'll write again tomorrow.

Love,
G.J.

15

12-25

D*ear Frankie,*

Forgive me for writing to you again. I know that you are busy amusing Surge and that hearing from me will only serve to remind you of our awkward farewell and the fact that my return (and thus Surge's departure), by the time you receive this, should be imminent. But the fact is, I may not return. If this letter reaches you at all, it may be months from now, when some summer visitor discovers our remains and my letters among them.

You see, Frankie, we are stranded on this deserted island. Charles Newet let our boat get away. We only have enough food for a few days. It is probable that we will starve to death.

Because I see my own death looming before me, and because too of recent events concerning the adults I am with (the details of which I will not bore you with at this time), I feel that I must let you know my true feelings for once and for all.

I love you, Frankie. But you are on a seesaw; you could go either way. I saw the look in your eye when you watched that murder movie at my house. And I've seen the look in your eye when you play with Surge. You've got two distinct sides, Frankie. Only the love of a woman like me can insure that you abandon one and develop the other to its full potential.

Oh, I know these words sound harsh. It's not your fault in the first place. You're male, so already the odds are against you. Did you know that ninety percent of all crimes throughout history were committed by men? I suppose it started back in the days when men were hunters and gatherers and women had to stay close to camp to keep an eye on the children. Naturally, your sex had to be aggressive, and genetic memory, apparently, has kept you that way, even though

138

we live in times in which such aggression is no longer necessary. Wars can be won with buttons nowadays, and if more women were in places of leadership instead of men, they might be done away with altogether, replaced with feminine warfare, which is to say negotiation and compromise.

And if it were only that you were male, you might still be able to defeat this thing, at its core at least, and emerge, as the majority do, with only an inflated ego and a propensity toward domination. But your father abused you emotionally, and physically too from what I gather. You've grown up motherless, in poverty, and with no self-esteem. It's only natural that you would look at the tough man in that awful movie and say to yourself, I want to be like that; if I were like that no one could do me any harm.

Let us save you, Frankie, Surge and I. If you keep saving your money, you should have enough by September to get that car you want so badly. Let's go away together then. We can start a new life, in Boston, if that suits you. I've applied to a few colleges there. We can live in an apartment off campus. You can finish high school and then I'll help you to get into a college yourself. We'll both work. The way you were that day in the mountains—so at ease—keeps coming back to me. The way you are with Surge . . . You could be a veterinarian, Frankie. Or an environmentalist. You could be any one of a hundred things. Let me be the mother who was taken from you. Let me be the sister you never had. Let me be your friend, your lover, your muse. I'll never use you, Frankie. I'll never hurt you.

And if the worst happens and I don't come back, then keep this letter with you always. Read it when you feel yourself drifting. Remember that there was once a girl who loved you and who offered to spend her life looking after yours.

Love,
G.J.

16

Dear Sharon,

I've done something awful. I hardly know how to begin to tell you about it. Once you've heard, you will surely want to add this letter to your other documents, but I beg you to resist the temptation. Burn it, Sharon, the moment you've read it.

In my own defense I can only say that I have not been myself— a complication that you of all people are bound to understand. I don't just mean since the day of the killings. As I explained in my two previous letters, for better or worse I fashioned a new skin for myself when I was forced to abandon the old one. And I was comfortable in it, more or less, until today.

Furthermore, I hardly slept at all last night. While the adults were up and about, it was easy enough to imagine that we would be rescued. But after I had finished your letter and then one other, and everyone, including Dad, had gone to bed, I began to feel certain that no one would come to rescue us, that we would die here, from starvation—or worse, by the hands of some pirates who may descend on the island in numbers too large for me to even consider holding them off with my acquisition, the nature of which there is no longer any sense in keeping from you. I have a gun, Sharon. And today I used it.

Ida awakened me very early, before the sun had quite risen. She must have had the same kind of night that I did because her little round face was full of misgiving and her eyes, which are generally bright, were dull. "I think we should go to the beach now," she whispered, "to see whether there are any boats about."

I reached into my bag, found my pad and pen, and wrote, Should we go to the sound side or the ocean?

She considered my question over the paper cup of orange juice which she had brought into my room with her. Finally she said, "We should probably awaken the others. Then some of us can go to the sound and the others to the ocean. We'll have to take matches and gather driftwood, then make a fire and pray it can be seen at some distance."

I followed her into the kitchen where we found Goliath rummaging through the cooler. She retrieved the remains of the chocolate cake, put it on the counter, and began to break off pieces with her fingers. She was dressed only in a T-shirt and black cotton panties. "I'm going to wake up Charles and Ed," Ida announced. "I think we should get out right away to look for boats."

Goliath shrugged and stuck a chocolate-coated finger into her mouth. Ida went to knock on Dad's door. "Right there," I heard him say in a gruff, startled, sleep voice.

Rousing Charles was not as easy. Ida stood at the door and explained about the watches in detail. I was still in the kitchen, so I couldn't hear his response, but it must have been negative because then Ida went into the room and closed the door behind her and a muffled argument ensued. In the meantime, Dad came in, rubbing his eyes with his fists. When he saw Goliath in her underwear, he coughed uneasily. Goliath only turned her back to him and continued to pick at the cake.

Charles came in with his arms crossed over his chest and a sour expression. He took a good long look at Goliath's backside. Meanwhile, Ida got down on the floor and used one of our cartons to draw a map of the island, as best she remembered it from our nautical charts, which had gone the way of our vessel. Some parts of the island, she said, were too dense with foliage to be gotten through, but about a mile to the north there was a break through which a few of us could gain access to the beach. The others, she thought, should go to the sound, not to the place where we had come in, but to a place west of it where there was a point extending out for some ways.

"I'll take the ocean," Goliath said, her back still to us. "The sound's too smelly."

"Good," Ida said. "Ginny and I will go with you and the men can go to the sound."

"Wait a minute," Charles said. "Maybe I want to go to the ocean."

"Oh, Charles, be gracious for once," Ida snapped.

So the three of us took half of the sandwiches that Ida had prepared
before waking me and walked to the ocean. We gathered broken
branches along the way and had the makings of a good fire by the
time we arrived. We prepared it, but Ida thought it best to wait to
light it until we actually saw something.

We saw nothing, Sharon. The beach was quite beautiful, but I
was in no mood to appreciate it and am certainly in no mood to
attempt to describe it now. Goliath, however, was so thoroughly impressed that she left Ida and me sitting on the sand and went off to
gather shells in the plastic bag that we had brought along to collect
our trash. We watched her go, her legs long in her cut-off jeans and
her gait as jaunty as a child's. When she had almost disappeared
from view, Ida turned toward me and said, "He did sound like a
man obsessed."

I don't think she was actually speaking to me. I think she was
speaking to herself and just happened to turn her head in my direction at that moment. Yet, she looked so tragic sitting there in her pale
pink sweatsuit with her arms wrapped tightly around her chubby
knees that I decided a response was called for and placed my fingers
gently on her forearm. She looked at me, her features scrunched up
miserably. "I want to go home," she whined.

I nodded sympathetically and then we both turned our gazes to
the horizon. In fact, we were so preoccupied with the hazy wavering
line where we hoped to see a vessel appear that we failed to notice
what was going on in the foreground. A returning Goliath informed
us. "Look," she cried. "Dolphins!"

There were several of them, and it was a curious thing, in view
of the rising tensions, to see them churning through the waves so
playfully. My inability to appreciate them (there was a time when I
would have gone out after them) only further depressed me. Goliath,
who had been running, was breathless. "Aren't they magnificent?"
she exclaimed. She put down her bag of shells, spread her arms, and
twirled, closing her eyes and inhaling deeply. Then she plopped down
next to Ida and put an arm around her. Ida scrutinized her. "He
did sound like a man obsessed," she declared.

Goliath seemed confused for a moment. Then she got it. "Oh, that.
I was only kidding him."

"No, but you were right," said Ida, a stream of tears running
down her glossy round cheeks. "I know Charles. He's a very linear
thinker. Very logical. He's not creative. He's not one to talk about

abstract concepts. The way he went on and on about how Ed should make his pirate woman obsessed, the way he groped for the words to express the extent of the emotion he thought Ed should endow her with. . . . well, that's so un-Charles-like.

"He said that Ed should make her unable to sleep, that he should make her toss and turn and wander about the decks. That's just what Charles does lately. I wake up in the middle of the night all the time and find that he's not in bed. It's occurred to me before, during these last months since we started having problems, that he might be having an affair. Everyone I suggested that to said I was crazy, that Charles would never do that to me. Now I know I was right."

"Did you tell Charles you thought that?" Goliath asked.

"Yes, I mentioned it a few times. He got very angry with me and said I had a suspicious mind. I thought he must be right and hated myself for having such a flaw. But now that I know that he really is . . . involved . . . with someone, it's a relief. You see, I'm not crazy after all."

"Oh, poor Ida," Goliath whispered, pulling her closer.

"I don't want to be like this," Ida sobbed. She bent her head and buried her face in her knees. "I don't want to be this weepy woman, this mushroom. I just want everything to be the way it was."

"There, there," Goliath cooed. "It'll all work out." Then she bent forward, so that she could see me. Mushroom? she mouthed.

I shrugged. Goliath smiled and I smiled back at her.

"I told him that once," Ida went on. "I told him that my well-being hinged on his love, and do you know what he said?"

"What, darling?"

"He said, 'Love, love, love, Ida. You have a beautiful house, a job you like, and two healthy daughters, and all you can talk about is—'"

"Shhh," Goliath said softly. "Don't get yourself so worked up. He's not worth it."

Ida wiped her tears with her sleeve. "I'm going to rinse my feet," she announced, and she got up slowly and began to walk toward the surf. Goliath, meanwhile, scooted over, so that we were side by side. To my surprise, she put her arm around my shoulders and squeezed. "Marshmallow, she must have meant," she whispered.

Though I knew the color was rising in my face, I turned to look at her. Her face was so close to mine that I could see a light spray of freckles, which I had never noticed before, parading across the bridge of her nose. She smiled a delightfully wide smile. "Your father's lucky. You're a beautiful girl, willful, and one day you're going to be a fine, strong woman," she declared. Then she kissed me quickly on the cheek.

I turned away, stiff and embarrassed, but Goliath only laughed. "Let's go down with Ida and stick our feet in the water," she cried.

Our plan, Sharon, was to meet the men back at the house in the early afternoon and report our findings. As we approached, we heard their laughter. We found them in the kitchen, sharing a bag of chips and drinking beer. "Ed thought he saw a mermaid," Charles declared.

"There was something sizable," Dad replied. "It moved the grasses in such a way that for a moment—"

"Did you see any boats?" Ida interrupted.

Charles leaned back against the counter. "Oh, didn't we mention that?"

"You saw something?" Goliath cried. "Did you light a fire? Did you get their attention?"

"Two young fellows in kayaks," Dad said. "They came down from the island just to the north of us. They're out now on the point having their lunch and resting up for the trip back. They promised to contact the Coast Guard as soon as they get there."

"We're saved!" Goliath cried. "Thank God! I was afraid I'd run out of cigarettes before we got rescued!"

Ida clapped her little hands together. "Oh, this is good news."

"We told them to tell the Coast Guard to wait until morning," Charles said. "That way we'll still get our two nights in just as we planned."

"There's still the matter of the boat," Ida muttered.

Charles threw a hand out at her. "Don't worry about the boat, Ida. I swear, you're never happy unless you have something to worry about. The boat will be found. And if it isn't, well, that's what insurance is for. Our worries are over. Let's all go to the beach and frolic in the sun for a while."

"I'm going back to bed," Ida replied. "I got up awfully early this morning."

Charles looked at Dad.

"I think I'll work for a bit," Dad said. "I had a few insights last night, into what it must have been like to live in the pirate community

on New Providence where Bonny lived for a time. I want to get them down before I forget them."

"Ginny? Rita?" Charles asked.

I shook my head and faked a yawn.

"I was at the beach all morning," Goliath announced. "I'm going to check out the island."

"Fine, I'll go to the beach by myself," Charles said.

Goliath disappeared into her bedroom and returned a moment later with the same cloth bag that she had had the first time I saw her. She slung it over her shoulder, opened the cooler, retrieved a beer and a hunk of cheese, and went out the door.

A moment later Charles left, carrying a beach towel, another beer, and the rest of the chips. Ida went to lie down and Dad went into the living room to set up his lap top.

I continued to stand in the kitchen for some time. I opened the cooler, but I didn't see anything in there that I really wanted. I went into my room, took out my writing pad, and began a letter to you, but I realized I didn't have very much to say. I went through my duffel bag next and retrieved the paperbacks I had brought from home. I read the review excerpts on the back of all three of them, and although they had seemed enticing enough in the store, I found I had no desire to begin any one of them.

I was feeling restless, Sharon, incredibly restless, so much so that it seemed to manifest itself physically, in my back and neck and shoulders. I realized that what I was experiencing was a hunger, a longing, one that I had not felt in so long that I nearly failed to recognize it. I put the books away, stuffed a towel into my shoulder bag, and hurried out of the house.

What I wanted, Sharon, was Goliath . . . , Rita . . . I wanted her companionship, her friendship, her warmth, her ability to see in me things I haven't seen in myself for so long. You must understand: I've been invisible. Perhaps you'll say I did it to myself, by taking a vow of virtual silence. I don't know; it seemed necessary at the time. In any case, with Mom so preoccupied with her own problems, Dad so preoccupied generally, and my newest friend having treated me roughly (a matter for another time), and you and Terri gone from my life, and not a friend, not a soul . . .

Then that moment on the beach, Sharon, when Goliath put her arm around me . . . she touched something in me, and for a moment

I escaped from the bubble that I have been living in, the bubble that I'd devised to protect myself.

I ran along the dirt path, breathless with my longing, exhilarated with my youth, free at last from my bubble, wanting to be reckless, like Goliath, to experience whatever might come my way, even if it hurt as much as . . .

. . . As much as it hurt to be there that day in the diner.

I ran with my mouth open, swallowing air greedily. Tears of bliss flew from my face. I went through a tangle of trees and caught, between their limbs, a glimpse of the sound. A cloud of terns was flying low above the water, their beaks pointing downward, their wings silver when they plunged, simultaneously, to strike their prey. It seemed a miracle, a thing of such great beauty that I thought my heart would burst with joy. The world made sense again, and I felt my blood pumping. My willfulness, which Goliath had discovered, seemed to emanate from my skin.

I thought I knew how it felt to be her.

The path forked, and I stopped to consider my next move. I was surrounded by low trees and I chose one and climbed up, standing so that my head protruded above the highest branches. The forest extended perhaps another fifty yards and then gave way to high grasses which became low sandy dunes and then the sound. Off to the southeast, I saw the kayakers, two lithe youths in bathing suits and hooded sweatshirts. One was smoking a cigarette, the other pointing at something in the water. I dropped down to a lower branch to watch them.

It was then that I heard Goliath's voice.

I turned quickly, eager to drop from the tree and run to her. But I heard a second voice, Charles's, and I froze.

They were coming along the path that I had taken. Intermittently, I could see the tops of their heads through the branches. "So when was this?" I heard Charles ask with an edge in his voice.

Quietly, I moved to a limb on the side of the tree opposite the path. I squatted there, my body tucked into a small ball. They reached the end of the path. There were only a few trees between them and me. "Last week," Rita answered. "I told him I'd think about it. Can you see anything?"

"It's not that far," Charles answered. "But we'll have to go through this mess first."

"Well, let's start," Rita said.

"We'll get all cut up."

"So?"

"So . . . if we both come back cut up . . ."

Rita sighed. *"Well, maybe we should head back then."*

"Don't do this to me," Charles said. *"You're so mercurial. You were the one who suggested this trip. You said we'd make lots of opportunities to be together. I didn't mean that we should turn back. I only thought . . . Why'd you tell him you'd think about it, anyway? Why didn't you just say no?"*

"Because I am going to think about it."

"Great. That's just great. And how long do you imagine it'll take you to decide?"

"I told him I'd let him know in a couple of weeks. And lower your voice. I'm not your wife."

"Rita, just tell him no. You know you don't want to do it. You can't. We can't go on like this otherwise."

"Why? What's the difference?"

"He's my friend. That's what the difference is. It's one thing with you seeing him a few times a week, but if you're living with him . . ."

"Oh, that's funny," Goliath said, *"coming from a married man. You can have it both ways but we're not supposed to."*

"Rita, please."

"Please yourself. I won't have you telling me what I can or can't do. I'm not Ida."

"No, you're certainly not."

"What's that supposed to mean?"

"Nothing, Rita."

"No, I want to know what you meant by that. Just what do you want, Charles?"

"I don't know. I don't know," he said wearily.

"Maybe we should just cool it for a while," Goliath said.

"Don't do this to me, Rita."

"Yes, Charles. That's what I think we should do. A couple of weeks. Until I've decided. You're driving me crazy. I can't make a decision about Ed when you're giving me a hard time."

There was a long silence, very long, perhaps five minutes. Then Charles said, *"Okay, okay, maybe you're right. Two weeks. Decide what you want to do about Ed and then we'll work out our own affairs."*

"Fine. Let's go back. I'm not having fun anymore."

"*And don't come to work.*"

"*What do you mean, don't come to work?*"

"*I mean for the two weeks, because that would only make it hard—*"

"*Does that mean you're taking me off payroll?*"

"*Payroll!*"

"*Yes, payroll. I have to live, don't I?*"

"*Rita, with the money I've been paying you—*"

"*If you take me off payroll, then I have no choice but to move in with him. I can't pay my bills, Charles!*"

"*Is that what this whole thing has been about? Money? I can't believe this!*"

"*You* can't *believe this!* I *can't believe this! You're threatening me, aren't you? You're forcing me to choose between Ed and my job.*"

"*You've* got *other clients.*"

"*You know I make peanuts off of them.*"

"*Stop! Stop! I don't want to hear anymore.*"

"*I won't stop.*"

Charles must have turned and begun walking away because Goliath yelled, "Wake up, Charles. You must have realized from the beginning that I was never going to feel about you the same as you did me. I didn't make any secret of it. I never exaggerated the way I felt!"

I dared to peek. I could see the top of Charles's head at some distance. He was running now.

"*If you take me off payroll,*" *she went on, shouting, "I'll tell everyone. I'll tell Ida and Ed everything! Better yet, I'll put you in a position where you're forced to tell them everything. I'll make you sorry you were ever born!"*

I heard branches snapping, and then Goliath appeared right beneath me, scurrying around trees, slashing at twigs with her hands, muttering to herself. When she cleared the trees, she stopped, and seeing the kayakers, began to run in their direction. "Hey," she yelled, her arms flying. "Hey, you!"

They had just been sliding their boats into the water, but they heard her and looked up. When she got close, they pulled their boats back onto shore. Then the three stood conversing, Goliath turning to point inland, probably toward our house. The taller of the two men pointed at his kayak. Goliath went over to it, looked into it, and said something more. Then the young man shrugged and held his kayak steady while Goliath climbed in. He got in behind her, a snug fit, to say the least. Then the boats pulled away from the shore, the lone kayaker moving gracefully, swiftly, while the other, the one with Goliath, had to break his stroke continually so that the paddle could be lifted over Goliath's head. Finally, she took it away from him and began to paddle herself.

I reached in my bag and took out the gun. You see, Sharon, in my mind, Goliath had not only betrayed Ida and my father, but me too, in some sense. I had counted on her to save me; I had thought that she thought me worth *saving. But this was a woman who had flattered a man into paying her a great deal more money, apparently, than her work deserved. If she had flattered me, I realized, it was for a reason. After all, I'm not beautiful and willful, am I? I'm a skinny little girl who looks like an eigth-grader, friendless, loveless, and afraid of my own shadow.*

I aimed the gun at her. I held it steady until she rounded the point and disappeared from my view. Then I lifted my arm, pointed the gun straight up into the cloudless sky, cocked it with my thumb, and pulled the trigger.

I was dazed, Sharon, lost first in the reverberation of the shot and then in the silence that followed. Somehow I managed to climb back down the tree. I started back up the path and was halfway to the house when I saw Ida and Dad running towards me. Dad's eyes were moist, something I had never seen before. "Ginny! Thank God!" he cried. He lifted me off the ground. "We heard the shot from the house," he said, his hands gripping my shoulders. "Do you know what direction it came from?"

For reasons unknown, I pointed toward the sound, to the place where we had come in on the boat. Dad turned to look. "Take her back to the house," he ordered Ida.

"Be careful, Ed," Ida called after him.

Charles was in the living room, sitting motionless on the edge of a chair. He looked at us when we came in. "Ed went to look," Ida said.

Charles slowly turned his head away. Ida sat down and lit one of Dad's cigarettes, something I had never seen her do before. None of us spoke.

Dad came back a hour or so later. "I didn't see anything," he lamented. "No boats, nothing. I walked all around the end of the island."

"*It must have been the kayakers,*" *Ida offered.* "*Maybe they shot at a duck or something.*"

"*It couldn't have been them. If they shot and then jumped right in their boats and headed out, they couldn't have gotten around the other side of the point in the time it took me to get out there. They'd have to have been in a speed boat to move that fast.*"

"*And no sign of Rita either?*"

"*No.*"

"*Oh my God. I hope she's all right,*" *Ida cried.*

"*She has to be all right,*" *Dad replied.* "*I'm telling you, there's no way that anyone could have left this end of the island without me having seen them. And if Rita had gone to the other end of the island, Charles would have seen her when he went to the beach. They left the house virtually at the same time.*"

Dad sat down hard in a chair and hung his head. "*Rita has a gun,*" *he said softly. Charles looked up abruptly.* "*I have no reason to think she brought it here with her—she keeps it in her apartment, in case of burglars—but she may have. She may have taken a shot at some animal, though God knows why she would do that.*"

We sat in silence, in the four chairs. My bag was on the floor, resting against my ankle. I imagined that I could feel the heat of my weapon on my skin. It made me uncomfortable. I got up, put the bag in my room, and returned to the chair again. "*It'll be time for dinner soon,*" *Ida mumbled. She forced a little laugh.* "*Knowing Rita, she'll be back in time to eat.*"

"*You don't know Rita,*" *Charles said slowly, cruelly.*

Ida and Dad looked at him. Then they looked at each other. "*Excuse me,*" *Ida said, and she went to her room and closed the door.*

Darkness came. Dad took a lantern and went out to look for Goliath again while Ida and I started dinner on the hibachi out in the yard. We could hear him calling her name, more and more faintly as he moved farther from the house. Charles stayed in the house alone, in the dark. Ida had fed him a tranquilizer, to divert the anxiety attack that she feared was coming, and left a lantern beside his chair before coming outdoors, which he hadn't bothered to light.

You may be wondering at this point, Sharon, why I didn't just tell them, if not what I'd done, at least that Goliath had gone off with the kayakers. Had I been thinking more logically, I might have. But it was beyond my powers of reasoning at the time to see how things might turn out or to guess what was in Charles's mind.

Dad returned and the three of us ate while Charles remained indoors. Ida said, "Suppose the person who shot the gun lives on the island? That would explain why you didn't see a boat leaving."

"I thought of that," Dad answered. He put his arm around me and some of the juices from his hamburger dripped down onto my sleeve. He noticed and released me again. "It's possible that someone's been holing up here, a criminal, an escaped convict or someone, and that Rita saw him and he, thinking he'd been found out, took a shot at her. That's possible."

"Oh, God, Ed!" Ida cried.

"However, it's not probable," Dad said quickly. "Like I said, she has a gun. It's more likely that she fired it and that now she's hiding."

"Why should she do that?" Ida asked in a shrill voice.

Dad stared at her, considerering his response. "I think the answer lies with Charles."

"What do you mean?"

He leaned forward and placed a hand on Ida's knee. "Ida, I don't know how to say this to you—"

"Don't say it then, don't say it," Ida cried. "I don't want to know."

Suddenly there was a scream, a loud bloodcurdling shriek. Dad jumped up immediately and ran to the house, with Ida and me just behind him. We found Charles in one corner of the living room, speechless, pointing towards the back rooms. Ida grabbed me and dragged me behind one of the chairs, pulling me down beside her while Dad made a quick search. "Nothing there," he said when he returned. Ida exhaled deeply.

"It was her," Charles cried. In spite of the tranquilizer he was quaking badly. "It was her ghost."

"It's time to talk, Charles," Dad said.

Ida lifted her fists and ran at Charles, beating him on the chest. "Did you shoot her? Did you shoot her?" she cried.

Dad moved forward and took hold of Ida's shoulders. Sobbing, she turned toward him and he wrapped her in his arms. Charles watched with something akin to horror on his face.

"Charles didn't shoot her," Dad whispered. "Remember, Ida? He was just coming into the house when we heard the shot? Do you remember that?"

Ida nodded. Dad waltzed her over to one of the chairs and made her sit down. Charles, in the meantime, was turning his head slowly from side to side, searching, I suppose, for Goliath's ghost. A scamper-

ing sound came from the kitchen and Charles gasped. "A mouse, Charles," Dad said disgustedly. "Now sit down."

Charles sat. Ida put her arms out for me and I went and squeezed into her chair beside her. Dad began to pace. "What happened, Charles?" he asked.

"I don't know. I was just coming in. You said so yourself."

"What happened, Charles?" Dad said much louder. "There may be some kind of criminal on the island. Our lives may be in danger. Rita may be lying out in the forest somewhere, hurt. Or she may have shot off her gun because she was angry. You have to tell us what happened."

Charles began to talk then, Sharon, with his head dangling, so that it took an effort to hear him over Ida's continual sobs. Listening to him reveal his secret made me feel justified in having kept my own. How else would Dad have learned the truth about the woman he had intended to live with or Ida about the man she had married? Charles's confession, reluctant, garbled, and veiled as it was (he mentioned nothing about Goliath's salary), was an absolute necessity.

He concluded his story, and for awhile we all listened to Ida's crying. Finally Charles whispered, "She said she would do something to force me to confess."

"Well, Charles," Dad responded, "I hate to offend you, but I find it hard to believe that a girl like Rita would shoot herself over you, if that's what you're thinking. I think it's more likely that she shot the gun off to make you think she did and that she's hiding somewhere now, perhaps in one of the other cottages, having a good laugh over what she imagines is going on over here. I can't speak for Ida, but for my part, I'm glad all this is out in the open."

Ida stood up so suddenly that I nearly fell out of the chair we had been sharing. "Let's look for her. I want to find her and kill her. We'll bury her here. No one will ever know."

Before anyone could comment, she collapsed onto the chair again and resumed crying.

Later, Dad took a lantern and went to search the cottages. Charles, meanwhile, went to bed, and I sat up with Ida, who simply could not stop crying. When Dad returned, Goliath-less, of course, and saw the state Ida was in, he suggested she go and get one of Charles's tranquilizers. Ida said she would rather die than go into his room. Hearing that, I got up myself, as I knew where the pills were. I had seen her fish out the one for Charles earlier, from a flowered case in her duffel bag. Supposing that Charles would be asleep after all this time, I didn't bother to knock. He wasn't asleep though; he was just getting up, and when I pushed on the door, we collided. I rushed past him and grabbed the duffel bag. As I was turning with it, he asked, "Did he find her?"

"No," I said.

He put his hand over his eyes and returned to bed.

We put Ida to bed in Dad's room, and Dad is on the second cot in mine. Since I don't hear any snoring (I'm writing to you from the floor in the kitchen), I assume he is still lying awake. Charles is not sleeping well either. I know that because every now and then I hear him gasp. Once he even yelled out, "No!"

There is a part of me, although a small one, that feels pity for him. I know very well what it is to have your dreams peopled with demons and ghosts.

Why am I telling you all this? you probably want to know. Well, here's what will be causing my nightmares tonight, if I ever calm down enough to go to sleep: Goliath will likely tell her escorts not to bother about the Coast Guard, that she'll go and tell them about us herself. But will she? What's to stop her from simply finding her own way home and forgetting all about us. She must realize that everyone here has turned against her. What has she got to lose? As we've already seen, she has no conscience, Sharon.

So I will go to sleep tonight, if I am able, with the same concerns as last night. We may starve here. You may never hear from me again. In the event that my letters are found, along with our bodies, and forwarded, you, at least, will know what really happened. Someone should know the truth. You, being its servant, are the ideal choice.

Lovingly,
G.J.

P.S. Tell my mother that I love her and that I forgive her for the way she treated me before I left.

17

Due to the nature of our trip, we canceled our rooms in New Bern and came back two days earlier than expected. I had wanted, more than anything else in the world, to fly right to Frankie's house, both to see him and to collect my beloved Surge. In order to insure that Frankie had not only received my letters but had also had time to consider the proposition I had set forth in the second one, I forced myself to wait the two days. Now, as I sat in front of the shack in the Yugo trying to compose myself, I happened to glance at the Stewarts' mailbox. There was no latch on the box. The flap was down and I could see the edge of my lavender envelopes beneath one larger white one. In spite of my efforts, I had still come too soon.

My stomach turned sickeningly as I considered pulling away and waiting another day. Then it dawned on me that my premature arrival might work to my advantage. If Frankie was rude again (I hated to think it possible, but I needed to justify breaking with my previous plan), I would have the option, which I knew in my heart I wouldn't use, of collecting my letters on the way out and saving myself from being made a complete fool. I took one final deep breath and pushed open the car door.

My approach alone should have been enough to rouse Surge, but I knocked for good measure. There was no answer; clearly, Frankie and Surge had already gone out for the day. Thinking that his father and brother must be out too, since there were no cars in the driveway, I turned away. I was half way back to the Yugo when I heard the door open. "Can I help you?" asked a none-too-friendly male voice, and I turned in response.

He stood behind the door just as Frankie had the first time I had come to the house. His face was thin and grayish, with hollow cheeks. The skin beneath his eyes was badly puckered. His lips, though, were Frankie's lips, and thinking that this man might well be my future father-in-law, I forced my brightest smile to my face. He didn't smile back.

"I'm Frankie's friend," I declared cheerfully.

He only nodded.

"I came for Surge."

The indignation left his dark eyes and was replaced immediately with confusion. "My dog," I explained.

"Oh, him," he said. "He's gone. Frankie took him with him. Wait a minute."

He closed the door behind him and then opened it again a moment later, holding a sheet of folded loose-leaf paper out to me. "He told me to give you this."

I stepped up to the stoop and took it from him. I opened it, but now *I* was confused and unable to make sense of the one line scrawled across the top of the paper. I folded it into quarters and stuck it into the pocket of my jeans. "When will they be back?"

"They ain't coming back, is my guess."

I could feel that I was trembling badly. It was clear where this was leading, but some part of me continued to cling to the notion that I must be mistaken. "Well, could you tell me where they went?"

"I wouldn't know that, ma'am. He didn't say."

"Well, could you tell me when they left?"

"Same day he come back here with the mutt."

"Well, then he must be at a friend's house. Do you know Tom Heely? Could he have gone to stay with him?"

He shrugged.

"How about his brother? Could he have gone somewhere with him?"

His features crinkled cruelly. "Frankie and Phil go someplace together?"

"Why not?" I whimpered.

He laughed, and I saw that most of his lower back teeth were missing. "They ain't talked to each other in well over a year!" he said, shaking his head at me as if this were common knowledge.

"But that's impossible," I stammered. "He's come to my house several times in Phil's car. If they weren't on friendly terms—"

"Old blue Chevy with one yellow fender?"

"Yes. Phil's car."

He stuck a bare arm out of the door and pointed down the road. I looked where he was pointing and saw the car in question in the driveway of another cottage some fifty yards away. "That's Miss Flagg's car. She's too sick to drive it anymore. Frankie was borrowing it from her in return for taking her to the doctor's every other Monday. She's got cancer bad. No hair left anymore. Not even eyebrows. It's a pity."

I gulped and fought to keep my tears in check. "So you're saying he stole my dog?"

He reined his gaze back in from Miss Flagg's house and wet his lips. "I ain't saying *stole*. Don't be going to the police or nothing like that with *that* word on your lips. He said it was an exchange, your dog and the money for the gun."

I gasped audibly.

"Cut his hand up too getting it for you, but he said you wanted it that bad, on account of some accident you been in."

"He stole my dog?"

"He bought himself a nice little pick-up with all that money you gave him. Your dog gonna be nice and comfy in the back there. Don't you worry about him."

"Please," I cried. "You must have some idea where he is. I have to have my dog back."

"I got to go now. I'm letting all the heat out of the house."

"But he must be coming back. What about school on Monday?"

"What about it?"

"Please, you've got to help me!"

"Nice meeting you," he said, and he closed the door gently. When I knocked again, he didn't answer.

I was crushed, devastated, crying so hard I could hardly see the road. I moaned aloud, giving no thought at all to the people in the cars that I passed. Finally I pulled off the road and vomited out the window.

The world was ending; there was no other explanation. I had become a talker again on the Coast Guard vessel, midway between the island and New Bern. I had had no choice. The others were too despondent to even notice that our captain was asking questions about our boat, let alone to respond to him. And now I had no one to talk to, no one who would understand. I had no place to go. Even my own mother, in fact especially my mother, was unavailable to me. She had gone and done just what she had threatened to do before I left for the trip. With the help of a psychic healer (who she said cleared out her chakras) and her therapist (who got her started her on Prozac, the effects of which she insisted she was feeling already) she had indeed become a new woman. I had known something was wrong back when I called her from New Bern to let her know that we would be back two days ahead of schedule. Her reaction, which should have been despair, was delight. In fact, she invited all of us, including Goliath, to come straight from the airport to the house so that she could hear all about our trip over the dinner she planned to prepare. I had to tell her then that Goliath wasn't with us, and that while I would pass on her invitation to the others, I doubted that any of them would accept.

Life was hell. The trip was bad enough, but since I'd been back, things were worse. Ida was staying with us, and she couldn't stop talking about what Charles had done to her. Mom, on the other hand, couldn't stop talking about how good she was feeling, with her drugs and her chakras spinning clockwise. Since Ida didn't want to bring Mom down, and Mom, likewise, didn't want to make Ida feel worse, I was the one they both wanted to talk to. They took turns coming to and going from my room, one bouncing in with ideas for her future, the other staggering in with the tissue box, declaring that she didn't know how she would get through the night.

And now my dog was gone.

I vomited once more and then sat in a kind of daze for a couple of hours. It began to snow, and I watched the flakes accumulate on the windshield. After awhile, I could no longer see out. I liked that, I liked the darkness in there, in the little Yugo in the middle of the day. But before long I found myself yearning for more darkness yet. I considered the trunk, but I could not visualize going outside to get into it. I looked over my shoulder, at the narrow strip of floor between the front and back seats, and then climbed back there and cried myself to sleep.

Usually when I dreamed about Beverly, it was about her death, but in the dream I had now she was very much alive. I recognized her immediately, because of the way her platinum-streaked hair caught what little light there was in the auditorium. She was sitting on a chair on the stage, all alone, dressed in jeans and a dark-colored sweatshirt. Her feet, however, were bare, and I was afraid that the floor would be cold and that she would be distracted by her discomfort and forget her lines. But she didn't, not a one, I knew, though I couldn't actually hear them.

My body was numb with cold and it took me some time to sit up and climb back into the front seat. I imagined that the Yugo was completely covered by now, and I was both sur-prised and disappointed when the windshield wipers quickly cleared what was actually there. It was dark, and I was hun-gry. More than that, I needed to be held, loved, reassured that Surge would somehow be returned to me, though I didn't know who would do it.

I drove slowly, in keeping with my energy level, which was nearly nonexistent, and allowed myself to become captivated with the snowflakes that were coming at me through the windshield. I hadn't seen my father since we'd returned from the trip. We'd come back from the airport in a taxi, because Charles's car, which had brought us there, had a flat tire. Dad and Ida and I had left him there in the cold to change it all by himself. While our driver was retrieving our duffel bags from the trunk, I leaned over to kiss Dad good-bye. He gave me his cheek, but didn't kiss me back. Before I got out of the cab he said, sternly I thought, "I want you to come over as soon as you settle yourself."

I hadn't settled myself yet, but if I waited to do so, I might never see him again. Now seemed as good a time as any.

I parked the Yugo by the Dumpsters and was halfway up

the stairs when I realized that I had left the lights on and had to go back down again. When I started up the stairs a second time, I had to use the railing to haul myself along, and by the time I got to the top, my glove was soaked and my hand frozen. I walked the catwalk slowly and in utter silence. If he wasn't home, I promised myself, I would simply lie down in front of the door and let myself freeze to death. My hand was numb now, and it wasn't such a bad feeling. In fact, it was nothing compared to the emotional ups and downs I had experienced recently.

Is this how it starts? I wondered. Are thoughts such as these—clear, buoyant, objective—a preface to suicide?

But he was home, of course. The night was so still that I could hear the tap tap tap of his fingers on his keyboard even before I opened the door. I stuck my head in and attempted a smile. Like Mr. Stewart, he didn't smile back.

He stood up and pointed to one of the chairs at the table, saying, "It's about time." When I didn't answer immediately, he cried, "You're not starting that stuff again, are you?"

"No, I'm talking." I sank into a chair, too cold, stiff, and tired to take off my jacket. I realized that I was still smiling— a melancholy sort of smile, I imagined—and I wondered if maybe my face had just frozen that way.

Ever the host, my father opened the refrigerator and took out a can of Pepsi and a couple of cheese sticks. The cheese sticks were wrapped individually, and as hungry as I was, I knew there was no way I could open them with my numb fingers. I wanted to convey this information, but I was feeling light-headed and didn't quite know how to go about it. The top of the Pepsi can was so icy I couldn't even imagine touching it.

"I'll get right to the point," Dad said.

As he was still standing, to my right and slightly behind me, I had to stretch my neck to see him. He was staring at my jacket hood, which, I suppose, was wet with melting snow. "I know what you did. What I want to know is why?"

"What'd I do?" I asked. My voice sounded like a little girl's, sweet and innocent.

He folded his arms. "You shot off a gun on the island. You let me run around in the dark like a lunatic looking for Rita's corpse. You let Charles spend one terrible night dodging demons. And Ida!" He threw his hands out and shook his head at the very thought of it.

"I'm sorry, Dad," I whispered.

"You're sorry! Is that all you've got to say?"

"Can I ask a question?"

He threw his hands out again and stood like that for a moment. "Go ahead, ask, and then I want some answers."

"Were you snooping through my bag?"

He turned on one heel and set his fists down hard on the edge of the counter. "No, I was not snooping through your bag. It never in a million years occurred to me that my daughter might be carrying around a loaded gun and might shoot it off and then not tell anyone even when she saw that the consequences of her action were driving certain people out of their minds and—"

"Charles deserved to be driven out of his mind."

He turned back towards me abruptly, his face red with anger. "And who the hell asked *you* to play God?"

"If you calm down, I'll tell you how it happened. But first I want to know how you found out."

"Accidentally," he replied. He sat down on his chair, rubbing one palm down over his face. "When I was sleeping in your room, your bag was by my cot. I woke up in the middle of the night and realized you weren't in the other bed. When I got up to see where you were, I stepped on it. I felt something hard. I couldn't imagine what it was. I reached down, to push it out of the way, and caught the gun by the barrel, and I thought, What the hell is this?"

It amazed me that in spite of the fact that the only thing on my mind was Surge, I was able not only to make sense of his words but also to respond to them. "But you didn't tell anyone. How come?" I asked.

"The shock of knowing that my own daughter was carrying a gun . . . Besides, Ida and Charles were sleeping by then. I assumed you were too, out in the living room or somewhere. The house was quiet and dark. There didn't seem to be any point in waking everyone up to announce that my daughter—"

"You thought I killed her, didn't you? Because she was your girlfriend and you knew I wanted you back with Mom."

"I never—"

"You did. If you hadn't, you would have told Ida and Charles in the morning, when we were waiting for the Coast Guard to come."

"You're wrong. I never thought that for a second," he insisted.

"You did, Dad. Ida woke up certain that Rita had killed herself. And Charles had been certain from the start. And the two of them were nearly nonsensical with the ramifications of that. Ida begged you to go and look for her one more time, and you just kept saying, 'Rita wouldn't do that. I'm not going to look for her because I know she's not dead. She's only hiding and when the Coast Guard comes, she'll come out.' But really, all that time, you didn't want to look because you were afraid that you would find her. I saw your face when the Coast Guard said that she had come in with the kayakers to say where we were. You were amazed."

Dad's head drooped over his computer.

"It's okay. You were just trying to protect me."

"I'm not going to have this discussion with you, Ginny. I never for a minute thought that. Oh, by the way, I removed your bullets. I forbid you to replace them. And now, *I* want some answers from you. For starters, where did you get the gun?"

"I borrowed it from a kid at school. He got it from his older brother," I lied. "It's registered and everything."

"Fine. You've got exactly twenty-four hours to return it to him."

"Okay." I pulled my gloves off and held my hands out to look at my stiff red fingers. Dad reached for the hand nearest him and held it. His head was still bent, and when I heard him sniffle, I realized that he was crying. I wanted to go to him, to comfort him, and to tell him about Surge and be comforted myself, but I was still numb, emotionally if no longer physically, and I couldn't bring myself to get out of my seat. Besides, to tell him about Surge, I realized, would be to contradict the lie I had just offered him. In effect, I *had* traded my dog for the gun.

I freed myself from his grip and began clumsily to peel the wrappers off the cheese sticks he had set before me. I popped the tab on the Pepsi and took a sip. Then I told him what I had overheard and why I had shot off the gun. He kept his head bent the entire time, shaking it almost imperceptibly. I tried my best, too, to explain why I hadn't told anyone that Rita had left the island with the kayakers, a considerable task since I didn't quite understand my motivations myself. "Are you mad at me?" I asked.

He lifted his head and looked at me so hard and long that I began to fidget. Finally he said, "I love you, Ginny. I'm sorry I put you through so much. I never intended it."

That my father loved me only made matters worse. It was too much to take, on such a cold night. It had come as a shock; in fact, I may have recoiled when I heard the words. It was easier somehow when I assumed he didn't really love me, when I thought he was too preoccupied to give it much thought either way, to have him living away from us, away from me, away from my day-to-day affairs, to know that he was eating without me, going to bed without first stopping by my door to whisper goodnight.

The truth, now, was unbearable, and one more infliction in an emotional body already so badly wounded that I thought I might explode. I was in the car again, driving again with my mouth open, trying to cry the way I had when I had come from Frankie's so that I could vomit again and then feel the emptiness that had followed my last expulsion. But however much I tried, I couldn't even bring forth tears.

I had a quarter of a tank of gas, and I was torn between the desire to drive until it ran out and a more logical but less intense longing to lie down in my own bed with my down comforter tucked tight around me. I had eaten nothing but the cheese sticks all day, and I was still hungry. As I headed towards the diner in town, I envisioned a scenario wherein my lasagna dinner was disrupted by an obviously drunken male. I pulled my gun from my bag to warn him away, but when he only laughed, I knew that he knew that my father had emptied the chamber. When I actually reached the diner and saw that it was bright inside, and empty except for one waitress who was staring out wearily at the snow, I decided not to stop after all.

Logic got the better of me and I headed home. The snow was falling harder now and the little Yugo kept to the road with great difficulty. I imagined that Frankie and Surge were in California by now, getting ready to spend the night on the beach. Surge had never been to the beach before. Somehow I didn't think he would like it.

I remembered all at once that my letters were still in the Stewarts' mailbox. I considered going back for them, but then decided that Mr. Stewart would likely read them and have a good laugh, which he sorely needed. If he passed them on to Frankie, so what? At best, Frankie might try to contact me, in which case I might be able to get my dog back. At worst, Frankie would have a good laugh too. Who cared?

I pulled into the driveway and turned off the ignition. When I'd left, late in the morning, I'd told Mom that I'd be back in an hour or so. The events of the day had been such that it hadn't even dawned on me that *she* might have needed the car, that she was probably worried sick about me after all this time. I stared at the door, wondering how long it would take her to realize that I was out in the driveway, expecting her to come stomping out, screaming about the anxiety I'd caused her.

I decided to stay in the car for a while, until the heat left it and I was cold and sluggish again. I was already dim-witted. My thoughts had been so clear and buoyant earlier in the day; now I could hardly grasp them. It seemed that they were being transmitted to me from someplace very far away. Miraculously, I recalled that Frankie had left me a note and that it was in my pocket. I removed my seat belt, unbuttoned my jacket, and retrieved it. My hands were already so cold that it took me some moments to unfold it. I turned on the overhead light. *Thanks, the clothes fit good,* it read.

"Thanks, the clothes fit good!" I said to the dashboard, and I threw my head back Goliath-style and laughed. I turned around to look in the back seat. "Thanks, the clothes fit good!" I declared.

I stayed turned like that, looking at nothing, imagining girls in the back, friends smiling in response to me and to Frankie's note. "Let me see that," I thought I heard one of them say.

In my mind I handed it over to her, and she read it and passed it around to the others. They all laughed, all my friends. *We* all laughed. Because that was what teenage girls did. They drove around in their mothers' cars in threes or fours or fives and they shared their experiences and their deepest thoughts and their plans for the future, and their troubles too. And then they laughed. And their laughter, coming all together like that, was a magical thing, and eventually it diminished their troubles. "Can you imagine?" I said to my laughing friends. "Can you imagine where my self-respect has been? Can you imagine, me, Ginny, writing love letters to a boy who nearly knocked me down when I went to kiss him? To a boy who would steal a dog from a girl who he knew very well was already emotionally damaged?" I threw my head back and shouted at the roof. "Thanks *yourself!*"

My friends laughed harder. *We* laughed harder. We laughed so hard the Yugo shook. Then, finally, the tears came.

They didn't last very long, however, because I happened to turn and notice that there was not one but two other cars in the driveway. One, of course, was Ida's Four-Runner. I couldn't say who the other belonged to because it was completely covered with snow.

My first thought was that it must be Charles. He had called the house several times, but Ida had refused to speak to him. I imagined that that was why my mother had not appeared at the door shouting that I was ten hours late getting the car back to her, and here she was worried sick. Charles had to be creating some scene in there for my mother to have forgotten all about me.

I opened the car door at once and marched to the house in the snow. If he was hassling Ida, I planned to throw him out. If he refused to go, I planned to show him my gun. Unlike the drunk in my diner scenario, Charles would be too stupid to realize that the chamber was empty. Charles, who was afraid of ghosts, would flee at once.

I was just reaching for the knob when the door opened and a woman appeared. She was wearing a dark red silk blouse and baggy pajama-style flowered silk pants. Her hair was pulled back into a bun, and her diamond earrings twinkled when she tossed her head. "Finally," she said, laughing. "We were making bets on how long it would take you to come in."

It took me a moment, but I recognized her. "Sorry about the car, Mom," I whispered.

She swiped at my concerns as if they were cob webs. "Don't worry about it. If I had wanted to go somewhere, I could have used Ida's. Come in, come in. We've got a lovely surprise for you."

I didn't think I could take another surprise, lovely or otherwise. I stood where I was with my lips moving in some absurd attempt to inform her of the condition I was in, but this lovely, cheerful creature who was my mother didn't seem to notice. She drew her head back from the door, to smile her lovely smile at Ida and Charles or whoever it was. I could hear music playing. Apparently they were having a party. Harry Chapin was singing, "All I've got is time, nothing else is mine, All I want is you and one more tomorrow . . ."

My mother, who was usually reduced to tears by this tune, closed her eyes, smiled, and inhaled deeply, as though to drink in Harry's optimism. If I'd had my wits about me, I might have reminded her of what had become of him. When she opened her eyes, she seemed delighted all over again to see me there. She opened the door wider and I stepped in.

Ida, who was sitting in the rocker, saluted me with her wine glass. Sharon, who was sitting on the sofa, released the peanuts she had just scooped up from the bowl on the coffee table and stood. "Ginny?" she asked in a squeaky voice.

"Sharon?" I squeaked back at her.

She was wearing her shabby brown raincoat, of course. The two heavy sweaters that she must have been wearing beneath it were now on the arm of the sofa. Her hair was longer, and her sneakers were new. Otherwise, she was just the same. "Sharon?" I asked again.

"See," said my mother, "I told you you'd be surprised."

I glanced at her, open-mouthed.

"Ginny!" Sharon cried, and in her attempt to get to me quickly she stubbed her toe on the leg of the coffee table and hooted with pain. Then she laughed, and then I was in her arms and everything was all right again.

18

We were up on the top of the mountain, lying on our backs on the ground in the very same clearing of the birch forest where I had come with Mom and Ida back in October the year before. Our heads were together, our legs out at angles like the spokes of a wheel. The sky was full of stars, and the forest was full of night sounds—if you listened hard enough. But we had arrived just before sunset, when the other hikers were quitting the area, and we'd had plenty of time to acclimate ourselves to the dark.

No one had said a word in some time. No one had moved. The waterfall could be heard in the distance, a mellow flow—there hadn't been much rain all summer. It was as mesmerizing a backdrop as you could ask for, and it was a pleasure to be mesmerized after the day that we had put in saying farewell to family and friends. The three of us would be sleeping at my house, and in the morning Mom would be driving us to Boston where we would be attending different colleges. Over the summer we had bullied our parents into agreeing to pay for us to share an apartment together for the first year. After that, we'd see.

"Are you sorry we didn't go to New Jersey?" Sharon asked, her voice as soft as butter.

"No, not really," I answered.

We had made our farewell list back in January, when we all got back together again and agreed that we would all go to school in Boston. At the time it had been months since I had even thought about Herman Gardener, but in the course of telling Sharon and Terri every single thing that had crossed my mind since we had gone our separate ways back in the fall, his name had come up. My desire to see him was revived and I added him to our list. Sharon, who still clung to her investigative ways, became so interested in pursuing the encounter that I didn't have the heart to tell her that my own interest was diminishing proportionally as the months went by. I had removed him from the list as recently as last week. I had my own father back now, emotionally speaking at least, and no need to elicit the concern of a stranger. "Can you believe my father?" I asked.

"Was that the first time you ever saw him cry?" Terri asked, referring to how he had broken down when we had been there earlier to say good-bye.

"No," Sharon said. "Don't you remember? He cried that night when Ginny was there telling him about the gun, the night Ginny found out about Surge."

"Oh, that's right," Terri said. "I'd forgotten."

"Surge," I sighed.

"The gun," Sharon sighed.

"We'd better get on with it soon," Terri said.

"Soon," Sharon and I answered simultaneously, but no one made a move.

We were silent again for a long time. Then Terri said, "Do you think we've grown up this past year? Do you think that what happened in September pushed us into adulthood prematurely?"

"Ah, a breeze!" Sharon whispered. We watched the fingernail clipping of a moon disappear behind a cloud and then reappear. "The forecast is for rain."

"Good thing you've got your coat," I teased her. In spite of the hour it was still very warm, and Terri and I were wearing only shorts and T-shirts. Sharon was wearing jeans, and she had her raincoat spread out over her legs, to keep the bugs off her, she'd said. I inclined my head towards Terri's. "I don't feel grown-up. I feel different, of course, but I wouldn't call it grown-up."

"And Ginny would know," Sharon added.

"How's that?" Terri asked.

"Well, while you were searching for the genie at the bottom of the bottle every night and I was pursuing new friendships so as to appease my therapist, Ginny was cultivating relationships with adults."

"You know very well," I said, "that the adults I spent my time with didn't show any signs of maturity."

"Well then, there's your answer for you, Terri," Sharon stated. "There is virtually no difference between teenagers and adults. None of us know what the hell we're doing."

"It's depressing to think so."

"No it's not. Not really. Actually, I think it's a contradiction in terms to say that someone is mature . . . or wise. You fall into a ditch, you scramble around for a while in the dirt, you figure out which way is up, and you emerge smiling and thinking you know something. Then you trip and go down and it starts all over again. The adults who appear to be wise are the ones who simply don't have any ditches in their backyards.

"Look at the Newets, for example. There they were, coasting along in their fancy house, blind to the fact that their daughters are abominable—"

"You never met them until today."

"Ginny told us. Anyway, the Newets seemed like wise, mature adults to me when I first met them. I remember sitting in your kitchen, Ginny, once when they were over, and we were talking about money—"

"Yes, I remember that."

"And Charles was saying that it was impossible to save money on a weekly basis from your paycheck, because all middle-class Americans spend every penny they make. That was when I'd gotten that $3000 from my grandmother and I wanted Charles to sell me a computer with a modem and the rest of it. And Charles said he wouldn't take my $3000 because I might not have a lump sum like that again for some time, and that the one thing you should never do with a lump sum is spend it. He said I should buy the computer on time and pay it off with my allowance and birthday money and baby-sitting money and so on. I took his advice and before I knew it, the computer was mine and I *still* had the $3000 to boot. And let me tell you, I thought Charles Newet was the wisest male adult in the world—after Ginny's father, of course."

"I see your point," Terri said. "So here Charles understood

how a large amount of money might never come one's way again but didn't see the parallel where Ida was concerned."

"That's right. He was prepared to empty his entire marital account for the sake of a . . . a . . ."

"Bimbo," I supplied.

"Bimbo. Thank you." Sharon said.

"Well, Charles was lucky, wasn't he?" Terri replied. "If today was any indication."

Our voices were smooth and low and inflectionless, like the voices of people in dreams. When we broke off again, to reconnect with the stars and the night, it seemed as if we had never spoken at all. Another cloud crossed over the moon, but this one was so delicately put together that it did not entirely diminish her light. When it had passed, Charles drifted back into my mind. He was the one who had come to the door when we arrived there earlier. He'd made us coffee and then he'd had us sit down in the dining room and tell him all about our apartment. Ida had been up in the shower. She hadn't realized we were there, and when she came down she was dressed in a bathrobe with a towel wrapped around her head turban style. When she sat down, I saw Charles's arm move; he had taken her hand under the table. Ida, who had been talking, stopped to giggle and then went back to what she had been saying. But Charles must have been doing funny things to her hand under there, because Ida's face got red and you could see by the way she kept biting down on the corners of her lips that she was trying not to laugh. They had reminded me of the Gardeners.

"Don't think it happened so easily," I said.

"What's that?" asked Sharon.

"Ida and Charles's reconciliation. Remember, I've had to listen to her all this time. I've had a blow-by-blow account of the forgiveness process, and it's not all that it's cracked up to be. I mean, when she first declared that she intended to forgive him and go back home, I thought she was some kind of saint. For a few weeks, everything *must* have been heavenly because I didn't hear a word about it. Then she started coming in to work depressed again, insisting that she was confused, not angry. She just didn't understand how after twenty-one years of marriage a thing like that could have happened, and unless she figured out *why* it happened, she had no reason to believe that it wouldn't happen again somewhere down the road. So Flo, the other woman at work, sits her down one day and tells her that it's natural for a man to pursue an attractive woman when he's been married for so long, that what Ida needed to do to insure that it wouldn't happen again was change her appearance, lose weight, wear makeup, buy some new clothes, etc.

"Well, all hell broke loose after that. Ida insisted that she liked herself just the way she was and if, after all this time, Charles was more interested in how she looked than who she was, she didn't want him anymore."

"Good for her," Terri said.

"Yes, but poor Charles. Here he was trying his best to patch things up. And here's Ida, so unwilling to do anything, appearance-wise, that might help things along, that she went quite the other way for a while. I mean, she gained ten pounds, on purpose. She started coming in in these rags that, my best guess is, she had used previously to dust her coffee tables. She stopped blow-drying her hair and let it just hang, and she was angry all the time. Not about Goliath, of course, because she'd promised herself that she would forgive him on that account, but about everything else that he did wrong.

"For instance, she bought him a shirt for his birthday and he left the box that it had come in up in their bedroom instead of throwing it in the trash. I can't tell you how many afternoons I had to listen to her describing how angry it made her to see that box sitting in the corner of the room. Finally I said, 'Ida, if it bothers you, why don't you just throw it out yourself?' She was all over *me* after that, saying that she was tired of picking up after Charles, that she'd been doing that her whole married life. He cut her badly, one big stab in the middle of the soul. But she got hers in too, little scratches every day until he was bleeding as well. She stopped cooking, you know. For months they lived on TV dinners. It was her way of punishing him."

"But her *intent* was to forgive him," Terri said, "and ultimately she did."

"She says it happened overnight, back in April, April 17, she says whenever she tells the story, and that's approximately once a week. She was having a terrible time with her allergies that day. That night, for no particular reason, which is sometimes the case, Charles had one of his anxiety attacks. So there they were, in bed, and Ida's dying with discomfort, with her inhaler going in and out of her nose, and Charles, who had taken his tranquilizer but wasn't feeling its effects yet, is shaking all over, and the bed is quaking, and they're both moaning and groaning. And all of a sudden it strikes Ida as terribly funny and she begins to giggle, and then Charles does, and they really look at each other, for the first time in months and months, Ida said, and then they're overcome and they can't stop laughing. Later, when Charles is all tranquilized and Ida's breathing properly again, one or the other of them laughs and they both get going all over again. It goes on all night; they keep waking each other up with their little snorts of laughter. And then in the morning, everything's fine. It's as if Goliath had never been born. They've been like two teenagers—Ida's simile, not mine—ever since."

"Incredible," Sharon said. "A simultaneous epiphany induced by shared physical trauma. It must be something like a simultaneous orgasm."

"I had an epiphany," Terri whispered, "back in January, regarding my . . . problem."

"And you didn't tell us?" Sharon asked.

"Well, it was back when you guys first started taking me to the AA meetings, when we all first got back together again. You guys were so happy to be helping me to get back on my feet that I was afraid that if you knew that something else had triggered my recovery, you might be hurt."

"Terri," Sharon said, "you have to stop projecting your own sensitivity onto other people. We would have borne it. Tell us now."

"Well, do you remember that first meeting that we went to?"

"Yes, it was held in one of the offices over by where Ginny works."

"Worked," I corrected.

"Well, the truth is, all during that meeting, while you and

Ginny were talking away, telling all those strangers all about our misfortunes on my behalf, I was sitting there thinking, *I hate this!* I hate this twelve-step business and I hate these slobbering drunks, and as soon as I get home I'm going to have myself a drink and forget all about this."

"Yes? So what happened to change your mind?"

"Well, then Ginny wanted to stop in at the church for a minute on the way out, to see how it looked all decorated with the stuff that the kids at the day-care had made. And I was—" She broke off to choke back a sob, then took a deep breath which rattled on the exhale. "It was moving," she whispered.

In fact, it had been; I had been moved myself, although not in the same way that Terri must have been. Ida and Flo had set up their display over in an alcove beneath a statue of Saint Francis of Assisi. They had put the fish on the floor and covered them with a crinkled blue-tinted cellophane that really did resemble water and that concealed the fishes' defects very nicely. They had created a bank for their "stream" with real rocks and tree trunks and clustered the little raccoons and bunny rabbits that the children had assembled around them, closely, so that you didn't notice their defects either. The horrible cardboard panels, painted to resemble mountains and sky, had been placed behind Saint Francis, but the wisps of clouds, angel's hair, which Flo and Ida had glued on kept you from noticing any flaws. The overall effect was glorious, truly. The pastor wasn't about, but he must have surmised that some of the AA people might come in, because he had a tape playing in the background, children's voices singing Christmas songs, both religious and secular. We came in in the middle of "God Rest Ye Merry, Gentlemen," and stayed until the end of "Winter Wonderland." So there, in the church, in the middle of that devastating winter, was the recreation of spring that Ida had envisioned from the start.

"I can't really explain it very well," Terri continued softly. "I can only tell you that something changed in me. And when I went home, I didn't have a drink."

"But there were episodes afterwards," Sharon pointed out.

"Well, yes, of course, and the AA meetings really did help a lot then. And I don't know what I would have done without you two throughout it all. But the children's display was the thing that enabled me to go forward with the rest of the process. That was what provided me with *my* intent."

Sharon sat up. "I think it's time. The moon's gone for good now. It's getting really cloudy."

I sat up slowly. It was like coming out of water after being submerged for a long time. Terri extended an arm and I pulled on it to help her into a sitting position. We spent a few minutes rubbing our eyes and stretching our legs, and then we all got to our feet and turned our headband flashlights on. I still had my father's and I had bought two others for my friends just for this occasion.

Sharon was the first to take up the shovel, but she hit some tree roots and had to start over again a foot or so away from the original spot. By the time she gave the shovel to me, the hole was already as deep as it needed to be, but as our ceremony called for involvement of all of us, I made a few token stabs at the earth and then passed the shovel to Terri, who did the same. Then we put the shovel aside, turned off our flashlights, and reached out in the dark to find each other's hands. Sharon, our designated spokesman, lifted her face to the dark night. "Spirits of the Night, Spirits of the Past," she called out in a clear loud voice that elicited a little giggle from Terri.

I squeezed Terri's fingers in warning and she whispered, "Okay," and then Sharon continued:

"We have come here tonight to tell you that while we understand the necessity of your persistence, we reject your implements as a way of life. Tomorrow we go forward, into the world of higher education, and, ultimately, adulthood. We refuse to be your daughters. We refuse to be victims of our own anger. Now, as a symbol of our renunciation, we return to you those things that are yours." She lowered her head and her voice. "Who's got the bag?"

We let go of each other's hands and Terri found the shopping bag that we had brought along and handed it over. Sharon reached in and pulled out the cardboard box containing her "documents." She had, in fact, made them up, her intention being to startle one or both of us into getting in touch with her in spite of the edict that she had laid down. Also in the box was the Faust play, which she had still never let either of us read. She bent low and dropped the box into the hole. "I am no longer angry with my mother or Dr. Lindsey for using bad judgment. I am no longer angry with Beverly Sturbridge for dying." She lowered her voice to a whisper. "And I am no longer angry with Thomas Rockwell." She handed the bag to Terri.

Terri cleared her throat. Fearing she might giggle again and ruin this for Sharon, who had conceived the idea, I nudged her. She took from the bag a wine bottle, which she had emptied one evening in May when she'd had a minor relapse, and dropped it into the hole on top of the box of papers. "I am a recovering alcoholic," she declared softly but surprisingly firmly. "I am no longer angry with myself for becoming one or with my parents for not noticing that I had become one. I am no longer angry with Thomas Rockwell." She passed the bag to me.

My fingers found Surge's spare collar and I had to gulp back the sob that threatened at that instant. "I am no longer angry with Frankie Stewart for stealing my dog," I said. I reached in again and took out the last item. "I am no longer angry with my father for hurting my mother and me. I am no longer angry with Goliath, for not being who she might have been."

I began to sniffle, out of nowhere. "Say it," Terri whispered. "It doesn't have to be true. You just have to *intend* it to be true for now."

"Leave her," Sharon said. "She will."

"I am no longer angry with Thomas Rockwell," I said, and I dropped the gun into the hole.

It hit the wine bottle of course, and we all jumped back from the flying glass. Then we turned our headband flashlights back on and bent over to cover the hole with dirt. When this was done, we straightened up and stomped on the dirt until it was level and hard-packed. "Well, we're done with that," said Terri as she rubbed her hands together to loosen the dirt on them.

"Ya hoo," Sharon replied.

Terri and I looked at her. She was beaming. Tears were flowing from her eyes. "Boston!" she declared by way of explanation.

Yes, Boston. It seemed real now. Tomorrow we were going to Boston, and our lives once again would be changed utterly.

"Ya hoo!" I said back to her.

Terri began to laugh. "You're regular Banshees. Is that the best you can do?"

"Listen to her," Sharon said to me. "As if she ever made a Banshee-like sound in her life."

"Do you think I can't?" Terri asked.

"No, I really can't imagine it."

Terri tilted her head skyward and took a deep breath. "I hope no one's listening," she said. Then she yelled, "YAAAAAA HOOOOOO!"

Then we were all screaming, screaming like Banshees, running along the forest path, stumbling over the rocks that our little headlights failed to illuminate, bumping into trees and into each other, heading for the parking lot, heading for adulthood, which, we already knew, was likewise a continual stumbling, a comedy of errors, and with no wisdom to be gained whatsoever.